# The Dangers to Hearts

**The Hearts in Hazard series ~ Book 6**

by

# M. A. Lee

WRITERS INK BOOKS

S

**The Dangers to Hearts**

NOTE FROM THE AUTHOR

This book is a work of fiction. The names, characters, places, and incidents are products of the writer's imagination or have been used fictitiously and are not to be construed as real. Any resemblance to persons, living or dead, actual events, locale or organizations is entirely coincidental. The author does not have any control over and does not assume any responsibility for third-party websites or their content.

Published in the United States of America

Cover by Deranged Doctor Design

www.writersinkbooks.com
winkbooks@aol.com

Acknowledgements

People who believe in your dream are to be treasured.

People who believe in your dream and actively support your pursuit of it are to be celebrated. **Diane and Steve,** I celebrate you for your constancy and effective encouragement.

You have helped my writing improve, my plots become interesting, and my characters become more appealing.

May the journey continue.


To **Deranged Doctor Design**:
Artistic designers and project managers who take a few words
and turn them into glorious covers.

Table of Contents

# 1811

Chapter 1 ~ Friday, 15 November

Ipswich

"Stay here." Jess handed the reins to his mother and hopped down from the wagon.

Mrs. Carter eyed the building. The back façade had boarded-up windows and dingy paint, far different from the street-facing front. "Jess, what is this place?"

The evening gloom lent a criminal darkness to the building. The back lane they were on hadn't pleased her when he turned the wagon onto it. Were she to know the place warehoused smuggled goods, she would be all for leaving and starting from scratch somewhere far away. "Just a building, Ma. I know the man who owns it. He might direct me to a job."

She nodded. Since they'd packed the cottage and left it as the sunrise lightened the sky, she hadn't asked many questions. A week past, and she still hadn't asked him the reason they had packed up and abandoned their home, not after he told her Palmer was dead. She had never asked about the smuggling he did with Palmer and Jem Webb. She had never asked about the freight he hauled regular to Ipswich, even though the Naze had never generated enough product to fill his wagon on such a regular basis.

She wrapped her heavy cloak closer. "I'll stay."

He entered the building without knocking.

The warehouse had never hived with activity. Today, though, it seemed empty of folk. A single light gave him the direction to the front. His bootsteps echoed as he wove between crates and barrels.

The lantern that guided Jess to the front swung from a hook in the center of the anteroom. More shutters covered the two windows. Off to one side of the narrow room was the man who fenced for the smugglers. He sat behind a big desk, positioned off to one side rather than directly across from the front door. A bottle of whiskey sat to his left. An inkwell with its quill sat before him. The room was barren of other furniture except for a handful of chairs, as nicked and scarred as the desk. When Jess emerged from the door to the warehouse, the man growled, "Far enough. State your business."

"It's Jess Carter, Mr. Helmes."

"Carter, is it?" The man lifted his hand from his lap. A gunmetal pistol remained pointed at Jess' gut. "Who else?"

The pistol confirmed everything he had ever thought about Dick Helmes. "Nobody," and he had the wits to add, "I got somebody waiting for me outside, in my wagon." He didn't name the person as his mother. Better not to tell the fence that he'd brought someone bone-honest to his warehouse.

"Ah. Another one of you who escaped the soldiers?"

"Yes." *Who else had escaped?* He had heard that the soldiers had arrested everyone at the Hawthorn Inn. He had slipped through the net because he hadn't returned to the inn. Nor had he waited around to hear the gossip before he got himself and his mother rolling with the dawn.

The pistol lifted. The lever released back into place with a click. "Come forward then. Let's see how you've survived the past weeks."

Jess dragged off his slouch-brimmed hat as he stepped forward. He dodged the lantern by cocking his head over. Helmes peered at him then nodded. He placed the pistol on papers scattered over the desk then rested his hand beside the grip.

"So, you escaped. Anyone else you know about?"

"Palmer died. Far as I know, everyone else was arrested, including Marthy Gilson."

"Ol' Marthy." Helmes grinned, revealing his gold-capped right eyetooth. He picked up the whiskey and drank from the bottle. Then he set it back down with a thud. "They'll be hanging the men and transporting Marthy and the boy, so I would think. Why are you here?"

"I need work."

"I'll not hire you. No one here in Ipswich knows my connection to Palmer and the rest of you. I'd like to keep it that way."

"So would I. I got out by the slimmest chance." He didn't add that the slimmest chance had amounted to saving Captain Farraday after Palmer had fallen to his death. No sense letting Helmes know that Jess had worked a deal to save his own skin. "I ain't looking to toss that chance away. I got nothing to tie me back to the inn, and the others will keep their mouths shut. I'm out of work since the arrests."

"And?"

The man wanted him to spell it out. Well, Jess had learned to read earlier than most. "You got a warehouse. I've got my freight wagon. I can haul for you, wherever you need, legit work, however you want it. Right now, I ain't even got a roof over my head."

"My need for haulage is greatly reduced, due to certain arrests."

"Fair enough," Jess allowed. He started to back out of the office. "We'll try farther north."

"Wait."

He stopped, hopeful. "You thought of something?"

"Maybe. I need to think on it." He picked up the bottle, eyed the amber liquid, then swirled it. Without looking directly at Jess, he asked, "What are you willing to do? You willing to work hard? Like on a farm?"

"I'm willing."

"I need to think on it," Helmes repeated. "Come back early tomorrow."

"I can do that. I can stable the horses where I always do."

"Do that. Bright and early in the morning." He saluted Jess with the bottle. "To new ventures," and he drank again.

.~.~.~.

Helmesford

Agatha wrapped her cloak tighter.

When she came in after sunset, Aunt Sally would cluck about the cold and the dark. Agatha, though, knew the farm to her bones. She would never get lost on her own land.

The sinking sun had painted brilliant colors, gold and pink, coral and orange. Not for the first time she wished she could capture the radiance on a canvas. She had neither the talent nor the skill. Her mother, may she rest in well-earned peace, had had both talent and skill, even though she'd been raised to a life of leisure. Her watercolors still graced the house. Agatha could only paint with the seeds she sowed and the harvests she reaped.

When there was a harvest.

The farm had struggled this year. When she had finally admitted that the workers wouldn't take orders from a woman—orders they hadn't hesitated to take from her as long as her bed-ridden stepfather was alive—she had hired a steward. And then another. And then a third. The first was a drunk. The second wasn't work-brickle. And the third—.

What could she say about O'Malley? She had yet to find a local lass who would claim the Irishman had forced her. Four had just giggled. The fifth had rolled her eyes and returned to her work. Agatha feared a crop of babies would fill the village next spring, and O'Malley would continue spreading his seed far and wide.

He'd tried nothing with her, but his obedience to orders was just a tad too ingratiating. He had a look that said he would plot to overthrow her authority, although he never challenged her directly. His mobile mouth often smirked with a hidden joke.

He had come to Helmesford with a recommendation from her cousin Richard in Ipswich. She suspected more than a recommendation between Richard and O'Malley. She had hesitated to hire the man—but she needed a steward the workers would listen to. The early fields were coming to harvest. More fields than she liked had never made it to sowing because the field men had refused to listen to her for the first time in years. Without her stepfather to back up her words, they just laughed and returned to their cider. She had pleaded. She pointed out their need for pay. She was ignored by the majority.

Oh, a few had come to work, or she would have no early fields at all. Her first steward Mr. Hurst stayed sober long enough to get many of the other fields plowed. The second steward Mr. Garner gradually saw to the planting of the plowed fields. And the third steward Mr. O'Malley steered them from first to last harvest. Yet Agatha had had to correct him several times on the order of the harvest. Surely the man could see when fields were ripened? Old Denny had shaken his head every time she had to repeat her orders to O'Malley.

She had pleaded several times this year for Denny to be her steward. The elderly man, however, wouldn't take the job that his knowledge deserved. He wouldn't give orders to his fellows.

The sunset colors faded. She needed to get off this hill and around the woods before the pitchblack night descended. *But what am I going to do?*

She took a last look over the farm then turned her back and headed down. Helmes House stood beyond the wood, its ground-floor windows lit against the deepening twilight. Aunt Sally would scold. Mrs. Cabot would threaten to quit again because she had to keep dinner waiting. If she could avoid Mr. O'Malley, then one thing might go right this evening.

Twilight turned to night as she skirted the woods. The path showed a lighter color, and she sped along, stirring up the masses of leaves. She stumbled a few times. She had stumbled so many times this past year, but not as much and not as seriously as in the year after her mother's death.

Full dark had descended when she left the wood's edge and ventured toward the farm buildings nearer the house. Old Denny's new pup barked as she passed his cottage. The fowls squawked and fluttered before settling back on their roosts. A cow lowed in the distant pasture.

She reached the kitchen garden. A dark shape separated from the bricked wall, and Agatha stumbled to a halt.

"Out past dark, Miss Helmes?"

"Mr. O'Malley. You startled me. Did Mrs. Cabot not send over your dinner?"

"I've had it. I'm looking for dessert."

"Dessert? Do you need to speak with me this evening, or can it wait till morning?"

He chuckled. "Always dodging back to the farm, aren't you?"

She had her feet under her again. "Well, Mr. O'Malley, you are the farm's steward."

"I'm surprised you managed a love affair at all, then, unless his talk of plowing got you excited. Was that it? You like your men to talk of plowing your furrows?"

She blushed and was fiercely glad the darkness hid it. "Have you been drinking?"

"Just cider. Not the fine stuff you keep in the house. I'm sure you shared that one or two times. At least once. Had to be, from what I've heard. Got your field seeded, then off he went, leaving you to face it all."

"What are you talking about?" Then she knew he'd heard about her two heartaches, lost love and lost child, and wished she'd kept her mouth shut. "How many fields are left to harvest, Mr. O'Malley?"

"You should know. You were up there counting them."

"If the weather holds fine—."

"If the weather holds, we got no problems."

"We should talk about the fields that lay fallow this year. We've never tried over-wintering here. My stepfather was intrigued by the idea—."

"We get the last feed in, I'm off to see your cousin in Ipswich."

She had successfully diverted his innuendoes and insinuations. She only needed confirmation that Cousin Richard had sent him for more than a single job. "And for what reason do you need to see him, Mr. O'Malley? You do not report to him, do you?"

He backed up a step. "Evening, Miss Helmes." And he walked away.

Agatha felt glee at the confirmation that his avoided answer meant ... only to be dumped into gloom. She couldn't fire him. Not yet. Not until the last field was harvested.

*What am I going to do?*

.~.~.~.

### 16 November 1811 ~ Ipswich

Jess pulled the wagon up in the same spot as yesterday. The early morning had not given any freshness to the back lane with its dingy buildings.

"Jess, I do not like this place."

"Nobody'll bother you, Ma, not this early."

"This man—he was part of the smuggling, wasn't he? It's the reason you don't go in the front door."

"That's over, Ma. You know that."

"I don't want you ruining the chance that Miss Katie gave you."

"It'll be Mrs. Farraday by now, Ma. Mrs. Farraday of Melton Hall."

"She gave you a chance, a good one. She kept you from rotting in gaol."

"I'm taking that chance, ain't I? But the world's a little closed when you don't know where to go."

"Melton Hall—."

"No," he said flatly and jumped down.

The warehouse's back door opened. Dick Helmes appeared. He hadn't shaved. His shirt-front under his jacket looked as stained as last night's. The smuggler's fence stared up at Mrs. Carter while Jess tried to crowd him back into the warehouse.

"Who's that?"

"No one you need to worry about."

"Wife? Girl you're plowing? She looks old for you."

"My ma," Jess said tightly, "and you'll treat her with respect. Even Jem Webb did."

Helmes laughed. "Mrs. Carter," he called and swept her a bow that conveyed mockery through its deepness.

Jess wanted to plant the man a facer, but he controlled it. "I'm here, early like you said. Did you come up with other work?"

He grinned, that gold tooth shining, and Jess wanted to hit him again. Whatever the scheme was, it would only benefit Helmes. "You said you'll work on a farm."

"Anything that's honest work."

"Now you're qualifying it."

"I don't do murder. I don't steal."

"Just smuggling."

He gave a clipped nod and didn't argue that those days were over. His ma had the right of it. Hard as it had been to find any work all the way to London and back, it was better than giving this man a hold over him.

"Happens that I know of a farm. Helmes House at Helmesford. Not much, just a manor and the acreage around it. Several fields, some pastures. A pretty situation that I want to keep an eye on. My cousin runs it."

"Harvest is nearly over."

"She'll take you on."

A woman in charge? He remembered the tight ship that Martha

Gilson had kept at Hawthorn Inn. He reckoned Helmes' age and figured an old spinster in her fifties would be particular about the people she hired and the jobs they did. But he was out of options. Winter was coming on. His mother needed a stable place, warm and safe. "She'll hire me at your word?"

"At my word." He produced a sealed letter and a loose sheet. Jess glanced down and saw a list of directions. "I got a man there," Helmes added. "The steward. Reece O'Malley. Make yourself known to him as my man. He'll set you and—your *mother* into a good place."

He reckoned he shouldn't bloody the nose of the man offering him a job. "My thanks."

"Oh, it's a tit for tat. I'll get what I need from you soon enough. For now, O'Malley's a womanizer. My cousin's a hard-headed woman. He'll have kept his paws to himself for a time. She's no looker. But with winter coming on, he'll be thinking of sticking it closer to home. You see that don't happen. You keep his hands off my cousin."

Jess winced at the crudity. "O'Malley ain't going to like my interference."

"Then he can go jump. It's my farm, soon as I marry Agatha and get rid of that trustee of hers. I don't plan to do that for another few years. You just get there, get connected to him, and settle in. I'll likely come for Christmas. It's traditional. And you'll be there making sure things fall my way, not his. You might even give them a push to help them fall my way."

"Yes, Mr. Helmes."

"Any questions?"

He had dozens, but none that this man wanted to hear. "No, sir."

"Directions clear?" When Jess nodded, Helmes said, "I'm surprised you can read."

"Ma taught me. I'll be on my way, sir, if there's nothing else."

"There isn't, Carter. You do what I said, and you got a place for life."

Jess turned away. The warehouse door slammed behind him.

As he climbed up to the wagon seat, he reckoned that Helmes offered the same thing that Jess had thought to have with the smugglers on the Naze—a place for life. But smuggling had led only to death.

What would this venture lead to?

Chapter 2 ~ Monday, 2 December

Helmesford

"Wait here, please, Mr. O'Malley," but the steward followed Agatha into the study. She didn't realize it until he shut the door.

Halfway to the desk she stopped and turned. He was closing the distance between them. She backed up, into the desk.

"I believe I asked you to wait in the hall." She wanted to kick her breathy voice that had lost its firmness.

"No need to wait."

"I *asked* you to. I tell you now to go back to the hall." There, that had the firmness she needed."

He reached her. She was a fraction taller than him, something she hadn't realized. When his eyes narrowed, she realized he also hadn't known that she topped him. That slight bit of superior height bothered him.

"I *order* you to go back to the hall."

"I'm already here." He came a half-step closer. "You have something you want to say?"

*Where are my wits?* She scooted to the side and swept around the desk. He followed, but she picked up one of the heavy ledgers and held it between them like a shield. "Indeed, I do. About the farm. We have not produced the yield we had last year."

"Not on my shoulders. I wasn't here when you planted."

"Yes, I know that. It is the yield, though, the harvest that we can send to the London markets, that determines what we can plant next year. Denny says we have the seeds we need for next spring, but I still hope for an opportunity to determine an over-wintering crop. My stepfather tried peas for a few years, but the field mice played havoc with the seedlings. Other farms similar to ours plant—."

"I didn't come in here to discuss crops."

"Yes, I know, but I fully intend to. A winter barley—."

He laughed and grasped the ledger. "I don't think so, Miss Helmes. Agatha."

"Mr. O'Malley, you do not have leave to use my given name." Rather than play tug-of-war, she ceded the ledger to him and darted to the other side of her chair.

He dropped the ledger. It thudded onto the floor.

"That's my stepfather's ledger!"

"So?" He rounded the desk after her.

She kept moving. "It's like a Bible for farming. His and his father's and his father's father."

"Should have had a son to give it to. I can give you a son." He stopped, standing where she usually sat to work. "I'm not chasing you round and round the desk."

"Oh, good." She stopped as well. Once he knew she wasn't going to fall into his arms, he should see reason. "Now that you've seen your error—."

"What error?"

She gaped. "Well, that I am not interested in an *affaire*, and—."

"You aren't tired of sleeping alone? You had your one fling, and that'll do you?"

Agatha bit her lip. He was burning bridges without a care for the consequences. "Mr. O'Malley—."

"Call me Reece."

"*Mister* O'Malley, I am not certain what rumors you have obviously heard, but—."

"I heard you had one beau. He got you with child and scarpered off. Nobody's touched you since. You got to be craving it."

"I cannot believe you have so completely misunderstood any of our encounters, Mr. O'Malley. But I would have you know—oh!"

Her cry came because he reached over the desk and snared her arm. With one yank he sprawled her half-across the desk. Both hands on her, he hauled her across the flat surface. Loose papers scattered. The inkwell dashed to the floor. The other ledger thudded off.

Kicking helped not at all, for her feet were behind her. He had her upper arms, and she could not get her hands up to gouge him with her nails. Shock controlled her longer than she would have believed, and his strength increased her shock. Not quite knowing how it happened, she found herself on his side of the desk. Before she caught her breath, his tongue was in her mouth. Still holding her arms, he trapped her against the desk.

Agatha jerked her head back and screamed.

O'Malley slapped her.

Stunned, she stared at him—until he tried to kiss her again. She shoved him. His tongue stopped her mouth. She bit it.

He flung her back. "Damn you." And his beefy hands reached to throttle her.

A big hand grabbed his shoulder and jerked O'Malley around. And a fist plowed into his face.

.~.~.~.

"I don't know as she's hiring."

His mother spoke into Jess' hesitation. "We were told we'd have a chance for work here."

The cook sighed. "Come away in. The miss just came through herself with the steward. You can wait in the hall through there."

Mrs. Carter gave a sniff. "Are your scones burning?"

"Dearie me," the cook cried, and Jess' mother gave him a push toward the hall.

He'd never been in such a big kitchen, with a huge hearth and cabinetry on all the walls. Then the front hall dwarfed any vision he'd ever had of such a place. The manor wasn't grand, but the woodwork gleamed, from the well-waxed floors to the large panels on the walls. A fancy-flowered vase sat on a marble-topped table in the center of the hall, just past the stairs that climbed from one side to the other. He thought it was marble. He touched a finger to the white stone with grey veins and found it cold. The paintings on either side had soft colors and edges. The one with the shoreline and cliff reminded him of the Naze. He stepped closer to peer at it.

Then a loud thump sounded from the room back off to the right.

Jess froze. He listened. Nothing.

He looked back at the painting—and voices began to penetrate. A woman's. A man's, rumbling a question. The lady and the steward, he reckoned, based on the cook's words. And the steward was O'Malley. They weren't his business, except as they could give him a job and roof over their heads. He had told his mother next to nothing about Dick Helmes' plan. She would have scowled when she heard the whole, so he neglected to tell her. He concentrated on the painting: a bright summer day, waves coming in, gulls flying. He could almost hear them.

The woman cried out.

Several more thumps.

Shattered glass.

Jess stopped hesitating. He opened the door.

A man held a woman, his mouth planted on hers while she struggled, trapped between the bigger body and the desk underneath her.

For one second he re-considered interfering. Helmes had said O'Malley was a womanizer. This could be a passionate embrace.

Then the woman jerked her head away and screamed. It was a weak sound, like she couldn't get her breath, but she definitely wasn't willing.

Jess started into the room. The slap to her face sped him up. She screamed again, her cry cut short when the man clamped his mouth over hers. Jess swore silently. If this were O'Malley, he was going to mill down the man that Helmes had wanted him to connect with. Dammit.

Of course, Helmes had also wanted Jess to keep O'Malley from putting his paws on his cousin.

The man jerked back, his mouth pouring blood. She'd bit him. Good for her.

He reached the desk as the man reached for the woman's neck. He jerked him around. The man's broad size warned him, so Jess hit as hard as he could.

The man went flying to his arse. For all his thickness, he came up fast and surged forward. Jess gave him an undercut then got three good blows to the belly. The man stayed down that time. He jerked out a handkerchief and held it to his mouth.

The woman came beside Jess. He glanced at her. Pale gold hair falling around her shoulder, pale skin, slim body. Almost as tall as he was, and he topped six-foot.

"I believe, Mr. O'Malley," she said hoarsely, "that you have received your marching orders."

The steward—ex-steward—looked up from the floor. He slurred something, the words smothered behind the handkerchief jammed in his mouth to plug his tongue's bleeding.

"You may clear your things from the cottage, please," Miss Helmes said, for it had to be Miss Helmes. "Be on your way within the hour. This gentleman here will hand over your pay for the rest of the month when you quit the farm. Do not let me see you again, Mr. O'Malley."

Jess kept a steady gaze on the thick Irishman, but he watched her out of the corner of his eye. She was cool, fighting off an assault and bleeding a man.

O'Malley climbed to his feet. He removed the soaked kerchief and spat. The bloody spittle landed on her grey skirt.

She didn't flinch. "Goodbye, Mr. O'Malley. Please give my best regards to my cousin when you report the reason you were fired."

Thinking of Helmes' introductory letter in his vest pocket, Jess swiveled as the man passed him. "Ma'am—Miss, you want me to see him out the house?"

She didn't respond.

O'Malley slammed the study door.

He glanced at her. She had gone white as her ruffled collar and leaned against the desk as if her props were knocked out. "I think I should—."

Her knees gave out. As the house door slammed, Jess caught her before she hit the floor. He swept her into his arms then looked around for somewhere to put her. Limp as she was, she would slide right out of the chairs. The window at the room's end had a bench seat. What did fine ladies use when they fainted? Smelling salts? Should he unfasten that high collar?

She stirred as he laid her on the bench. Her body was light, her limbs long and slender. He tried not to look at her pale hair, like spun gold and falling loose. And her pale skin, so pale he could see the purple veins on her eyelids. And her mouth, more luscious than the rest of her slim form. Full lips, all reddened from O'Malley's assault. He shouldn't be thinking about kissing her himself, not after—well, he shouldn't be. She was all pale, like an air-spun angel—except for that mouth. Especially when her lips moved.

She was no ancient spinster, that was sure.

"Did I just swoon?" she asked faintly.

Jess cleared his throat. "Not quite a swoon. More like a here and there and back again." He slipped his arms from under her. Strangely, she clutched at him, her fingers grabbing his coat. Felt like she clutched at his heart. He stared at her fairy-slim hand and cleared his throat again. "You got whiskey?"

"Yes. I do believe I need some," she said, her voice strengthening. "Sit me up."

"No, not when I ain't here to catch you. Lie still." He spotted the whiskey. He unhooked her hand, laid it on her flat stomach with a pat, and went to the side table.

He splashed whiskey for himself as well and drank it down while he carried hers back. Setting his glass on the desk, he crossed to her.

She had shut her eyes again, but her lids fluttered open when he stopped beside her. She struggled up. He was quicker with an arm behind her back to lift her. Then he held the whiskey to her lips.

She sipped, swallowed, and coughed.

"More."

Obediently she sipped and swallowed and managed not to cough this time. She lifted a hand to cover his. Her fingers were icicles. "I can hold the glass myself."

"Your hands are shaking. Another."

She drank again then said, "No more, please," and he believed her since she was asserting her will. He remembered how fast she had recovered from O'Malley's assault, only to swoon once the man was out the door, so Jess stayed close.

He set the glass on the floor then scooped her up, turning to sit on the bench and settle her onto his lap.

She stiffened. "What are you—?"

"You're shaking like the last leaf on the tree. Be still. It's no more than I'd do for any child that's had a fright."

She shuddered. "A fright. Yes, that's what it was."

Jess held her chilled body firmly. He was now breaking Helmes' requirement about "hands off". Helmes might have meant O'Malley, but Jess knew the Ipswich fence had intended Jess to keep any man away from his cousin.

His young cousin.

He grinned, because she couldn't see it, then sniffed her hair. Lemon verbena. He remembered her periwinkle eyes staring at him, wide with shock. She didn't look nothing like Kate Charteris, and she stirred him more than Katie ever had.

She shifted again. "I do think I should get up."

"What did I tell you? Be still."

"I am a spinster of more than thirty years, sir, not a child who needs cuddling after a fall."

He sighed. "Am I assaulting you?"

"What? No. But—."

"Then be still." Fine tremors still quivered through her. She felt cold against him. He said the first thing that came to mind. "Maybe I need to hold you, you thought of that? It's not often I come on a man assaulting a woman. Congratulations, by the way. You did good, biting his tongue."

Her shudder this time wracked her harder than the previous ones had. "I fear I only made him angry. Oh, God," and on that she burst into tears.

Jess turned her a little, opened his coat to get her cold body up against his frame, and held her tightly. He grounded her with touch and heat while she dissolved into the tears she'd managed to stave off longer than he'd expected.

She also stopped crying faster than he expected. She hiccupped then began searching for something.

"What is it?"

"My hanky," she whispered.

He gave her his. Any dainty thing she had would be soaked before she dried her cheeks. Pink now, he noticed. He wondered how long she would perch on his lap before she realized his arms no longer surrounded her. She gave a last dab to her eyes then folded her hands on her lap and looked down.

"You rescued me and—and rousted the dragon and have let me cry on you, and I do not even know your name." Those periwinkle eyes peeked at him.

"I'm Jess Carter," and then he lied, "and I don't know your name either."

"Agatha Helmes."

"A pleasure to meet you, Agatha Helmes."

"And you, Jess Carter."

*What now?* he wondered.

"I am sorry that you found it necessary to rescue me."

"I'm not." His retort brought her lashes up again, rewarding him with another look from those pale fairy-flax eyes. Her eyes lifted again, rewarding him. "I have an ulterior motive, Miss Helmes."

Before he could explain, the door flung open, and a windstorm in a red cape came in.

"Agatha! I just passed Reece O'Malley heading to his cottage. He was all bloody."

Agatha Helmes nearly fell off his lap. Jess steadied her then gave her a little push to get her standing. Caught sitting on his lap, she blushed as bright as the woman's cape. She stepped forward to meet the woman as Jess stood. He remained at the window bench, though. Here was the older spinster that he had expected.

"Who is that man? Why were you—have you been crying? You have! That Mr. O'Malley, I am certain. It's time you were rid of him, Agatha."

"I fired him."

"Good. But now we need another steward. I suppose his firing did not go smoothly?"

"He tried to—." She stopped, unable to describe O'Malley's attack.

"He assaulted Miss Helmes," Jess put in. He tried to ignore the two cats stropping his ankles, claiming him by rubbing their scent on him.

"And you routed him?" The older woman clapped her hands. "Excellent!"

"Miss Helmes bit his tongue."

"Famous! I will write *that* to Marilla. She will be pleased. She has looked for O'Malley's removal since she met him a month ago. Now, who is *this* man, Agatha?"

"This is Mr. Jess Carter. Mr. Carter, this is Aunt Sally, Miss Sarah Wellesley. My step-aunt, really, but she's closer than the rest of my blood relatives." The two women smiled at each other.

The older woman was not a Helmes, Jess realized. Dick Helmes' cousin was Agatha Helmes, the hard-headed spinster that the man had said was no looker. She was definitely a Long Meg, and so pale in color and hair that she would look colorless next to a vibrant brunette. Yet Jess didn't think she was ugly.

The red-caped whirlwind had finished looking him over. "Aunt

Sally will do," she told him, casting aside his one attempt at social forms. "Are you not on a first-name basis with Agatha? She was sitting on your lap."

"Aunt Sally!"

"Miss Helmes was crying, Miss Wellesley. I did no more than offer comfort."

"And his handkerchief." She looked at the crumpled cloth in her hand. Her face crumpled up, ready for more tears. Jess was ready to wrap an arm around her. He was curious how her aunt would deal with her crying.

"Young man, it will have to be Aunt Sally whether you like it or not."

"Yes, Miss Wellesley."

The older woman gave him an arch look then turned to her niece. "You need tea, child. That will steady you."

"I had whiskey," she offered, and yet another view of this woman fascinated Jess.

"I'll tell Cabot," the older Miss Helmes said and marched from the room. The calico cat started after her. The marmalade one prowled away from the desk, picked a spot before the fire, and settled down. Purring soon filled the room.

Agatha Helmes darted a quick look his way then began to pick up the scattered papers. Jess put the ledger back on the desk and picked up the ink well. The glass bottle had broken into three pieces. Spilled ink had stained the silver and poured onto the floor. One corner of the stand was dented. A beautiful thing, now marred forever.

When she came to the desk, he handed the silver stand to her. She reached for the broken glass, but he pushed her hand away. "You'll cut yourself."

"Throw the pieces into the dustbin there under the desk."

He saw the copper bowl, but it wasn't in him to just toss something that could be repaired or remade. "You might could have another inkwell made up."

She didn't sort the papers, just hastily stacked them and slid them under the ledger. "I don't want to look at it for the rest of my life and remember this day."

He chucked the pieces. Then he took the silver stand and chucked it as well. "That ink is going to stain the floor."

"I can live with that stain. Shove the desk over it or something. You—you handled my aunt well. She is rather forceful."

He just grinned.

Agatha Helmes looked relieved. She fiddled with the stack of papers. "You said that you had an ulterior motive for coming here."

He would have to sidestep Dick Helmes completely. "I was told you might have work. We're looking for a place."

"We're?"

A cry of "Ah" was heard. Even from a distance, joy filled the sound.

"My mother and me. She's waiting for me in the kitchen."

Agatha compressed her lips. "The job of steward is currently available."

Jess shook his head. "I can't take that one, Miss Helmes. I don't know farming. By trade I'm a freight hauler with some time spent on boats. We lost our home, and we just ... decided to move on. Greener pastures."

"Helmes Farm certainly has several green pastures."

Her persistence won another grin. "I can turn my hand to most things. A bit of carpentry and such. I got a strong back and plenty of stamina. Whatever you put me to, I won't be quitting it on you."

"Mr. Carter, my aunt Sally is right. We are far past first acquaintance. So, Jess," and her cheeks pinked as she daringly used his first name, "I will have to consider what job I have available for a man of your worth. You may be assured of a position. That I promise."

"My mother will need work as well, Miss. We'll need a roof over our heads."

"You will stay here tonight, Jess, you and your mother." Here was the hard-headed woman he had expected. Her tone would brook no objection. Even when he tried, she waved aside his protest. "You are my guest tonight, for—for routing the dragon."

She left him with only one thing to say. "Thank you, Miss Helmes."

The door opened. The cook came in with the tea tray. Aunt Sally followed with a three-tiered tea stand. Behind her came his mother, bearing another tray.

Jess exchanged a look with his mother, the smallest flicker of his eyes, a slight tilt of his head toward the younger Miss Helmes. She compressed her lips, a recognition that she would keep her mouth closed about their personal business until they could talk privately.

Chapter 3 ~ Monday, 2 December

Agatha held back as Aunt Sally managed the seating, giving Jess the largest chair, her late brother's. *Mr. Carter*, she reminded herself with no expectation that she would be able to walk back to the formality of his surname.

When she took her usual seat, she realized she sat closest to this man who hadn't been in Helmes House more than a half-hour but already belonged to it. She gazed curiously at Mrs. Carter, who was near to Aunt Sally's age.

Delilah, the calico, crawled under Jess' chair—*see, you can't return to his last name.* Mrs. Cabot poured the first cup of tea. Agatha found herself eager for the bracing liquid.

And Jess swore softly.

Mrs. Carter and Aunt Sally gasped. Mrs. Cabot paused in the act of handing his mother a steaming cup.

"My apologies. I left my horses and wagon—."

"Mrs. Cabot," the older woman interrupted, "would you have Denny see to Mr. Carter's wagon? You can send little Mike to fetch him."

The cook sniffed but retired to her kitchen while Aunt Sally picked up the teapot. "There. Cream and sugar, Mrs. Carter?"

"My son takes his tea black. I like a drop of sugar, please."

"Excellent." She passed the tea to Mrs. Carter who passed it on to her son. The cup and saucer were dwarfed by Jess' big hand.

The calico stretched her paws around Jess' foot, protected by his leather boots. She patted his ankle, not sinking her claws in, as was her habit with others who came to tea.

"You need not worry," Aunt Sally was chattering on as she poured Mrs. Carter's cup then added a little spoon of sugar. "Denny will take excellent care of your horses, and he'll leave the wagon at the stable."

Here was something Agatha could talk about that wouldn't bring up O'Malley or her silly swoon. "What breed of horses do you use for your wagon?"

"Shire." He accepted a plate with a savory pasty and a buttered scone.

"We have the Suffolk Punch as well as the Shire for work on the farm."

"The Shire can haul more weight. That's needed in a dray animal."

"We like the Punch for its stamina." She liked his brown eyes, the fall of his brown hair over his high forehead. He had a long thin nose to go with his lanky form and a sharp chin. She had once thought she preferred a square chin on a man. That had been a great mistake.

"Yes. The Punch can do the plowing and harvesting you need."

"Exactly. Have you always had the Shire breed?"

"Excuse me, Agatha," Aunt Sally interrupted and proceeded to pepper both Jess and his mother with a series of questions even as she pressed more pasties and scones and a slice of cake on them.

Until Mrs. Carter put down her plate with a decided click. "I cannot hold one bite more, Miss Wellesley. A fine tea, Miss Helmes."

"I find your scones delightful, Mrs. Carter," her irrepressible aunt said.

Agatha took a new look at the buttery scone that she was gobbling up without thinking. She shared a look with her aunt. "These scones are much better than Cabot's usual recipe."

"Forgive me, ma'am and Miss." Mrs. Carter had a direct look, a manner that Jess had likely picked up from her. "I have fair enjoyed our talk, but I would be wondering if you have any jobs offering, anything suitable for my son and myself."

"I have offered the steward's position to your son, Mrs. Carter. Perhaps you can help me persuade him to accept it?"

"That will be a decision for him, Miss."

When all eyes turned to Jess, he said, "I have no farming experience."

"I do," Agatha said immediately. "I have run this farm for the last three years, since my stepfather was crippled. Before then, we would consult over what was happening on the farm, what needed to be done and what decisions had to be made. I only hired a steward because the workers would not take my orders after my stepfather died."

"They thought Agatha only conveyed my brother's orders," Aunt Sally added. "But many times, especially in his last year, he wasn't able to think what to do. The workers refused to take orders from a woman, fools that they are. She would stand in a field with them, listening to the problems they put forward, and when she gave them the solution, they ignored her. They didn't ignore her when my brother was alive."

"If O'Malley was entrenched here—."

"He wasn't. He only came here a few months ago." Agatha's shoulders slumped. "The third failure. The first man couldn't stay sober six days out of seven, and the other—well, he wouldn't keep to work and the morning would be half-gone before he showed his face."

"I don't know—."

"I can tell you what needs to be done. Old Denny, he's been here since he was a boy. He will help you, too. Most of the workers have no trouble taking orders, but a few—."

When Agatha faltered, Aunt Sally stepped into the breach. "I suspect her cousin in Ipswich, that Richard Helmes, is undermining her. He's always wanted this farm."

"We have no proof, Aunt Sally."

"No proof, but that's the only reason for—well. I don't understand his reason for interfering, but I have no doubt he keeps fingers on the farm's pulse point. If I could determine how, that would be a good day's work. We hired O'Malley on his recommendation, hoping the problems would stop. O'Malley's presence barely put a dent in them."

"Problems?" Jess sat forward and put his empty plate on the little side table between him and Agatha. "What kind of problems?"

"Men wanting paid although they didn't finish the work. Men refusing orders. Fights breaking out when we've had none before. A circle of workers got involved in gambling and complained that they'd been set up. Mr. O'Malley said it wasn't worth getting to the root of those problems."

"It would be worth it," Jess said, "if you can weed out the trouble-makers."

Agatha smiled, and was surprised when he blinked like she'd blinded him. "Already I prefer your way of thinking to Mr. O'Malley's. Will you take the position, Mr. Carter? Yes, I know you don't know farming, but I do. If you are willing to accept my guidance and direction, we can work very smoothly together, I do believe." Her direct look willed him to accept the offer. He'd been an answer to her earlier prayer for help against Mr. O'Malley. She prayed he would be another answer to prayer. The farm didn't need another year like the last one.

He dangled a hand over the arm of his chair to let Delilah bat it with her paws. "I just take your orders and see they're carried out?"

"Yes, only that." When she named the wage O'Malley had received, his mother's indrawn breath proved that they had never seen such money. For her trump card, Agatha added, "As part of that wage, the steward gets a cottage here on the estate." She didn't add that the cottage would be the perfect place for him and his mother, but she couldn't resist a little more. "There's a shed for your wagon, and I'll pay you anytime you use your horses for work. It wouldn't do for a pair of Shire to get fat and lazy."

For some reason he reached inside his vest and touched whatever rested in an inner pocket. "Let me speak with my mother about this. It's a step in a direction I wasn't expecting."

"Your mother is right here."

"Aunt Sally, he means that he wants to talk to his mother in private. They would be able to talk about reasons without our overhearing."

The older woman sat back in her chair and folded her arms. "Caution is sometimes wisdom, sometimes folly."

She frowned at her aunt and tried a smile on Mrs. Carter.

That woman returned it. Her brown eyes shined. Her apple cheeks gave her a merry look. Agatha wanted to get to know the woman. But she didn't dare press more than she had.

She had laid out a clear argument for Jess to take the job. The decision had to be his. "Would you be able to give an answer by morning?"

He glanced at his mother then gave Agatha another level look. "Yes. By morning."

"Good." She stood. "I need to get the pay I promised to O'Malley. Are you willing to give it to him when he comes to the house for it?"

Jess flexed his right hand as if he would be willing to give the big man another helping of his fist. "Yes, Miss Helmes. I'll do that, no trouble. And see him off the farm if you want."

"I don't think that will be necessary." She tugged on the bell pull. "Cabot will clear the tea things. Aunt Sally and I will see to your rooms for tonight. And your mother and you can collect your things from the wagon. Little Mike can show you the way. Ah, Mrs. Cabot, you were quick. Will you tell Little Mike to take Mr. Carter and his mother to their wagon? They are staying the night with us."

"I'd like fine to have known that earlier."

"It has just been determined. Thank you, Mrs. Cabot."

The cook grumbled but led them out.

Aunt Sally managed to wait until the door shut. "You let Cabot have too much leeway. She would never have said that in my brother's day."

"Quite a lot would never have been said or have happened in my stepfather's day. And while I can do many things, I cannot cook. Nor can you. Mrs. Cabot has to stay."

"I think Mrs. Carter would replace her. Did you taste her scones? She saved the tea."

"Aunt Sally, please think above your stomach."

"The stomach drives the heart. Why do you think the proverb says 'the way to a man's heart is through his stomach'?"

The idea of Mrs. Cabot's removal was tempting, and Agatha contemplated having breakfast without having to hear sour comments. But she shook her head. "I do like Mrs. Carter. She doesn't put on false airs."

"The way the doctor's wife does. That woman." The orange tabby mewed and pawed at her skirts. The older woman scooped him up and settled him on her lap. He purred when she rubbed his brow. "The cats like Mr. Carter. They didn't like Mr. O'Malley. Did you see him play with Delilah? Delilah likes so few people."

"She didn't like the other two stewards," she mused. She had watched Jess drop his hand down beside his chair. He had dangled his fingers to tempt the calico into play.

"She doesn't even like the vicar, and they have that fat grey cat. Delilah sank her claws into the vicar last week."

Agatha considered the past half-hour and more. The speed of O'Malley's assault, the quickness with which Jess had despatched him, followed by his kindness in dealing with her weak sobbing. And then a cozy tea as if none of the other had happened. It seemed unreal.

"Am I jumping too fast? I have offered this man the job of steward for the farm. I am not going to consult with Mr. Camden, my trustee. It would take too long. A steward's job is one of great trust. I know nothing of him, of his background, of his work habits. I know less than nothing."

"You must know something, or I wouldn't have found you sitting on his lap, with his arms around you."

"Aunt Sally, be serious."

"I am serious. He defended you, obviously, or O'Malley's wouldn't have sported that bloody nose and swollen eye. He comforted you. He did not take advantage when a lesser man would have. Am I correct? That seems a better recommendation than the one your cousin gave for Reece O'Malley. Mr. Carter may prove stubborn, however. You must underscore that he needs no knowledge, only the ability to lead your workers and gain their trust."

"We know nothing of him, of his past. He could be evil. He could be a criminal running from arrest."

"His behavior wasn't evil, was it? He looked us straight in the eyes. He carries himself well. Not like a shifty criminal."

"Aunt Sally, you have never seen a criminal. How would you know how they behave?"

"I have an imagination, don't I? And neither of us would know what an evil man would look like."

"I do. I fell for Stanton Myers, and he abandoned me. We both mistrust my cousin Richard, but we hired O'Malley on his recommendation."

"Let's wait and see. We'll find out soon enough what kind of man he is. Denny will let us know."

.~.~.~.

Jess handed a satchel down to his mother from the bench of his freight wagon. Slinging another one over his shoulder, he jumped down. His mother nodded toward the stable. A hunched man was hobbling out of the stable, following a little boy.

The man stopped and eyed them both. The years had weathered him brittle and dry, an ageless age that could range from the seventies through the eighties. "Yer the Carters, the boy says. I got yer horses in stalls, rubbed down, watered. I'll see to their feed later, if you like."

"I appreciate that. I would like to check them over. We had a long haul today."

"Aye, yer a good horseman, then. But just a moment, sir. Go on with you, Mike. Yer mither'll be wantin' to go back to the village." Leaning on his muck fork, he waited until the boy scampered back toward the house, and Jess watched him warily, wondering what the old codger wanted to say. "I hear O'Malley's gone and you're the one what rousted him."

Jess shrugged. "Miss Helmes was holding her own when I came in. She bloodied him."

"But he's gone now, and here you stand."

What should he say? Did the old man support O'Malley? "We're looking for work," he cadged.

"Steward's job?"

A good start never happened with a lie. "Miss Helmes has offered it. I'm considering it. My ma needs work as well. We heard Helmes Farm had jobs."

He gave a nod to Jess' mother then fastened his little eyes on Jess. "Heard that, did you? Few farmin' jobs around in the wintertime, and here we are at the first of December and needin' workers. You know anything about farmin'?"

"Kitchen garden for my ma, repairs around our former place. I'm a wagoner by trade. The name *is* Carter."

The old man grinned, showing missing teeth. "Independent wagoner's a hard job. Smaller routes are left, but the big firms in London have taken the paying routes. That why you came here? Looks like your whole house up on that wagon."

"One of the reasons."

"Helmes Farm suits most of us. Miss Helmes treats us fair."

"Even though she's been through three stewards? She told me that herself," he added when the old man's brow knotted down.

"No fault of her own. She's a good 'un for all her past mistakes.

That man she got rid of, he'd an eye to the main chance. She stuck with him because the other two were worse. All of them sent by her cousin. He's sendin' trouble, I'd say, even without evidence. He wants her in debt to him. Gives him a better hold on the farm." He leaned over and spat. "You going to take steward?"

"I haven't decided."

"And that answer's got me thinkin' yer the one for the job. Our Miss Helmes, she knows the farm. She just needs a man to run it for her a few years, till her cousin stops stickin' his fingers into a pie that ain't his. Where you staying for the night?"

"Up at the house."

The bushy white eyebrows lifted. "Now that's a surprise. She must've took to you. And her Miss Wellesley agreed. Now that one's a piece of work, all the Wellesleys are. You need help cartin' what you need up to the house?"

"We can manage."

"But we thank you for offering," his mother quickly added.

Denny nodded. "Yer wantin' to see your Shires. Come on then."

The old man pointed down the stable. Jess saw his horses peering over the stall doors. They looked content in the box stalls, munching hay and swaying on their feet.

After patting down his horses and checking their hooves, he returned to his mother to find she had pulled a second bag from the wagon.

Jess took the heavier bag from her. When she tugged at another, he took her arm and turned her toward the house. "This is all we'll need tonight."

They walked back. He saw his mother looking around the neat enclosures, the kitchen garden with its protecting brick wall. Then she lifted her eyes to the manor house, with its three stories and three double-set windows on the first floor. His gut clenched at the question he knew was coming.

"Will you take her up on that offer?"

"I'm not a farmer," he repeated his argument.

"She said she would guide you. That man said she's fair. This could be the place for us."

"I know you're tired of traveling. We left the Naze more than a month ago. Don't fasten on a place just because it looks comfortable."

"It's more than the way it looks. I liked Miss Helmes and her aunt. They were both friendly. Neither one put on airs. And that old man said Miss Helmes is fair."

He thought of Agatha's light weight on his lap. He remembered the sweet smell of her, the creaminess of her skin, the periwinkle blue of her eyes. That frowsy hair. And her mouth——. Jess jerked his attention back to his mother. "You like it here?"

"I could like it here, especially if I spent time in that kitchen. Did you see it?"

"Just when I passed through. I wondered if you would be entranced when you saw that range."

She sighed. "The Self-acting Kitchen Range. I read about them. They can heat a lot of boiling water and keep two cooking plates hot all the while roasting a bird, with no additional fuel!"

"Heaven."

"It is! You should know from the quantity of coal you had to haul for me when I was taking in laundry."

"And it entranced you enough to try it out with your scones."

His mother sniffed. "Mrs. Cabot burned hers. And I will admit to being entranced by that range if you will admit that Miss Helmes entranced you."

"Ma, I just met the woman for the first time barely two hours ago."

"I know my son."

He didn't argue with her. His attraction to Agatha Helmes was the stronger of the two reasons he didn't want the job of steward. Even as she drew him in, he knew nothing could come of it. She was gentry-born, just like Kate Charteris. He would wind up heart-hurt yet again. Instead, he reminded her of the cousin. "We've got a problem."

She sighed. "Your connection to Richard Helmes in Ipswich. It seems like he's not the recommendation he thinks he is."

"If she discovers my connection to him——. Hell, if she finds out I've hauled smuggled goods to him and I've escaped the law myself by the veriest luck——."

"Not luck. You did the honorable thing on that cliff, the right thing, and Miss Charteris rewarded you for it. There is no law on your tail, Jess."

"But it's a lot of reins to keep untangled. We might be better served moving on, letting go of all our ties to the past."

"You can never let all of them go. Just when you least expect it, someone from your past will find you, and it's all there again, in ways you can't control."

His mother sounded as if she spoke from experience, but she wouldn't tell it. She never spoke of her past before she met his father and made a life on a headland slowly crumbling into the sea.

"You think I should take this job of steward?"

She stopped and stared at the house with its creamy walls and dark green shutters. "I do, Jess. Whatever you don't know or understand, admit it to her. Be up front with her."

"Even to my smuggling days? Even to my criminal association with her cousin?"

"The smuggling, yes. It will explain the reason we left everything. If she don't like, it, then we'll move on. Tell her first. See her reaction. Then take the job she's offering."

"If she's still offering it. You wouldn't tell her about Helmes?"

"No, say nothing of him. She's not thinking highly of him right now."

"And admitting to a crime is safer?"

"Not safer; wiser. And you know it, my son."

Chapter 4 ~ Tuesday, 3 December

Agatha Helmes was definitely a long Meg, and she presented herself at the breakfast table in attire designed to keep Jess thinking of her as a spinster. She'd raked her pale hair into a tight bun and wore an ugly wool dress that hid her womanly assets. With glasses perched on her thin nose and her collar buttoned up to her swan's neck, she looked as severe as any village school mistress.

Then her aunt teased her, and her lips melted into a smile while her purply eyes sparkled, and Jess wondered again how she'd gone unplucked for so many years.

He followed her into the study, puzzling over his interest in her. Matched against Kate Charteris, Agatha Helmes was barely a spark. She matched him for height. Folded on a ledger, her slender hands had overly long fingers. Hollows beneath her eyes and in her cheeks gave her a pinched look. Then she smiled and transformed. Her fairy spell enchanted him again.

"Have you come to a decision?"

"You honor me with your offer, Miss Helmes, especially since I've got no one to recommend me."

"I thought we agreed on first names, Jess."

He tightened his lips.

She blinked at him from behind her pince-nez. "Your actions recommend you."

"That sounds fine, but there's two problems."

"Two problems shouldn't be insurmountable."

He frowned.

"I will be quiet," and like a child she locked her lips and tossed the imaginary key over her shoulder.

Jess cleared his throat. He agreed with his mother's assessment, but his aversion to telling part of the truth nearly gagged him. "The way you described the job was you giving the orders and me getting the workers to do them. I don't know farming. I'm a wagoner." He said the next quickly, hoping he didn't stumble over the one lie he had to tell. "We heard you were needing people. I was thinking it was for a short patch, through the winter maybe, and then I'd be back to my business. I had a route in and out of Ipswich. I had to give that up. Wherever I go,

I'll have to find new people to work for."

"Jess—."

He held up a hand. "Let me get through this. You need to know it all. Steward's a position of trust, and I ain't sure I'm a man for you to trust. The reason we left home, the reason I've not got a route in and out of Ipswich, well, the short of it is that I hauled for smugglers."

Her face froze. He'd known it would. She didn't frown, she didn't smile, she didn't gape at him, she didn't do anything. "Smugglers?" she whispered.

"They trafficked with France. Got themselves involved with a French spy. That got them arrested. I ran the sails for them some, not much. I didn't get arrested, and I *know* there's no warrant out for me, but I had to cut ties and leave. We're starting over, my ma and me. I won't work for you unless you know what I've left behind. Now, ask what you want, and if you want us off the property, we'll go, no complaints."

"You hauled smuggled goods into Ipswich?"

"Yes."

"Did you ever meet a man named Richard Helmes in Ipswich?"

Here was his lie, and she had fastened upon it immediately. He stepped carefully. "I know the name. I've met the man. We're not mates." None of that was a lie, but he had a foul taste in his mouth.

"How do you know there's no warrant for you? If you cut ties and left while the arrests were going on."

He hid his sigh of relief that she moved away from Dick Helmes. "The man who was hunting the French spy, I saved his life. I went against orders to do it. My reward was getting out with my name still clear."

"Is Jess Carter your real name?"

"Yes."

"You have given me much to think about." She looked down at her hands, clasped tightly from the moment he started his first concern. She unclasped them and flattened them on the closed ledger. "You only want to work for the winter season?"

"No, I'd like the steward position."

Her head lifted. Light sparkled in her eyes.

"It's up to you, Miss Helmes, whether it's today or tomorrow or next week or never. You tell us, and we'll leave. Or hire us and we'll help you with the farm."

"You haven't told me anything that changes my job offer, Jess. If anything, what you've said has confirmed that you are deserving of my trust and this position."

"You should think about what I've told you."

"I will," she promised then proceeded to enlighten him on the jobs that a steward oversaw during December. Her only concern seemed to be if he would tolerate taking orders from a woman. Remembering Marthy Gilson's whipcrack orders at the Hawthorn Inn, Jess didn't see any problems taking Agatha's soft-spoken orders that sounded more like questions.

She did blink when he asked about moving into the steward's cottage.

"Did Mr. O'Malley receive his last pay from you?"

"I gave it to him, aye," along with some well-chosen words about making himself scarce.

"Do you mind—if my step-aunt and I can impose upon you a little while longer—both of us felt safer last night with your sleeping in the house. Would you mind delaying your move to the cottage? It is an imposition, I know."

"It's not an imposition, but it won't look right to—."

She talked over him, giving him a taste of the hard-headedness her cousin had warned him of. "And it will give your mother time to give the cottage a thorough cleaning before you move in. I know a few village woman who might be willing to help, even with how busy they'll be as we all prepare for Christmas. Would your mother be willing to delay the move?"

He could only think to say, "We'll be making extra work in the house."

"Not that much. We barely have enough for Tassie now. She comes in for the daily work, and her sister Posie comes in twice a week. Do ask your mother if she'll be comfortable here in the house for a few more days. Shall I see if Little Mike is at hand to take you to Denny? You did meet Denny yesterday?"

She was rolling faster, and he knew she did it to keep him from protesting her request that they stay in the house. "We did meet Denny. I liked him. He's the kind of man I'm used to. But, Miss Helmes, about staying in the house—." The words of refusal died on his tongue when her eyes widened. She had paled, if creamy skin could go milk-white. "Are you afraid O'Malley will come back?"

"I wouldn't put it past him." She sounded firm, but he saw her hands shake.

"Very well, we'll stay in the house a few nights, until he's had time to leave the district and my ma's had time to clean the cottage. Now I should see Denny. He can tell me how best to meet the other workers."

"The local pub—."

"Yes, I'll go there, but I want to meet them one on one, when they're working. And Denny will ensure news of the old steward's firing spreads. No details. Just the bare deeds. If they're loyal to Helmes Farm, they'll be offended that he laid a hand on you." *The old man might also know if anyone was stirring up trouble behind the scenes.* Jess touched his temple as he rose from the chair across from her.

He drew on his knitted cap as he left the study.

His mother puttered in the kitchen garden, ostensibly peeking under cloches to check for any fresh greens growing, for they were warmed under the glass. When she saw him, she straightened and wiped her hands on her borrowed apron. "What did she say?" she hissed.

"We're staying."

"You told her?"

"Pretty much everything, including that I knew her cousin in Ipswich. She still offered the job. She said my honesty about the smuggling and hauling smuggled goods was a recommendation." His wonder at her words colored his voice, and his mother's eyes widened. "We've got one hiccup—she wants us in the house for the nonce."

"In the house?" she squeaked.

"She says it's because she's worried O'Malley will come back. She says that she and Miss Wellesley feel safer with me in the house. She probably just wants to keep an eye on me."

"That's good sense. That O'Malley doesn't sound like a good man. What's for you today?"

"I'm off to Denny and to start learning the winter work on a farm. Which isn't much different than your kitchen garden, just much more acreage to do it on. And you?"

"I'll sort through the wagon and get most of our personal things to the house. Miss Wellesley has offered to show me the steward's cottage this afternoon."

"You'll be here then or at the wagon or at that cottage?"

"Don't worry about *me*. I can take care of myself. Off with you."

.~.~.~.

Monday, 23 December

The days passed and became a week, two weeks, then three. The weather turned colder, the ground harder. Aunt Sally began her decorations for Christmas, and her two cats batted around the paper chains and sniffed the evergreen boughs. Delilah pounced on Little Mike when he ventured past the kitchen. Little Mike had to be comforted with a sugar cookie, and the affronted calico stalked away, tail high.

Agatha watched the Carters. The steward's cottage repaired and cleaned, Mrs. Carter had inquired only this morning when they could move. Agatha had promised tomorrow. She was reluctant, for they helped the house feel not so empty. Jess' presence seemed to ground the house, just as her stepfather Robbie Wellesley had grounded it during his nine years as man of the house. *The manor needs a man*, she thought fancifully only to scold herself for thinking that.

Mrs. Cabot found her after breakfast. "Miss Helmes, I'd like a word."

Aunt Sally looked up from another paper chain. "When did Jess say he would bring in that tree?"

"This afternoon. What is it, Mrs. Cabot?"

"I didn't protest when you let them Carters stay the night. You know I didn't."

"Indeed, and I appreciated it, Mrs. Cabot. Have you found Mrs. Carter a helpful addition to the kitchen?"

"She's always interfering. Don't I think a little bit of sage on the chicken crumble? Or a bit of thyme on the beef? She's always adding something."

"It is eye-opening to try new flavors, don't you think?"

"The thing is, Miss Helmes, how long are they going to be in the house?"

"The cottage roof did need repairs, Mrs. Cabot, and that led to repairs needed in the two first floor chambers. Those were only completed last Wednesday."

The cook folded her hands over her stomach before she countered with "The thing is they could have moved to the cottage and back since last Wednesday."

"I believe they were still painting those rooms on Saturday. Would you have them move on the Lord's Day?"

"No, Miss Helmes. The thing is—."

"I did tell Mrs. Carter that they would have help moving soon. Tomorrow is Christmas Eve. We would not want such an uproar over the holidays, would we? We can all help them to move after Boxing Day, can't we?"

"The thing is, Miss Helmes, I didn't hire on to cook for a passel of people. I thought I'd be cooking for just you two ladies—and myself, of course. The thing is, even after they move, they'll be up here at the house, taking meals all the time—."

"Certainly not breakfast."

"No, but it'll be tea and dinner and maybe supper and who knows what else?"

Agatha hid laughter. "I don't believe there are many meals beyond the four we've mentioned." Aunt Sally didn't hide her snort.

Which provoked a sniff from the cook. "The thing is, Miss Helmes, I've heard from my sister in London. She's got a house and rents rooms. She's offered to pay me for my work."

"I pay you, Mrs. Cabot."

"Without interference in my kitchen."

Ah, Mrs. Carter's apple cheeks were probably glowing. The woman was the better cook, and her recovery of Mrs. Cabot's meals was becoming a daily occurrence. Relief flooded Agatha and left a cozy spot, for now she had a position for Mrs. Carter, tying Jess and his mother more tightly to Helmes Farm. And she refused to examine that wish. "You're leaving us, aren't you, Mrs. Cabot?"

"I am, Miss Helmes."

"At Christmas?" Sally cried, and Delilah hissed. "You are abandoning us at Christmas?"

"Yes, Miss Wellesley," the woman said without hesitation. "The thing is I'm packed and waiting for the cart to take me to the village for the mail coach. You'll need to send my trunk to this address." She fumbled it out of her pinny and laid the paper on a nearby table. "I'd like my pay now, Miss Helmes."

"Of course. You must have planned your removal to your sister's for some time."

"She did ask me to come in October. I wrote her that I'd take her position, if 'twere still open, the second day that the Carters were here."

"If they have offended you, or if we have—."

"No, Miss, just being in the kitchen when I'm cooking."

"I did think Mrs. Carter was helping."

"She helped, Miss Helmes. The thing is I've been thinking about a change for some time."

"Should you need a reference—."

"I won't, Miss. Thank you, Miss. That'll be the pony cart now."

"Then I had better get your pay. And your Christmas bonus." Agatha hurried upstairs to the lock box she kept in her bedchamber. With the Christmas rush upon them, she had already set aside the little Christmas stipend in envelopes for the chief servants she relied upon. When she returned, Mrs. Cabot stood in the entrance hall. The open door admitted the cold air. With her black hat tied under her double chin and her black cloak about her, the cook was a shapeless mass. "Here you are, Mrs. Cabot. Happy Christmas and best wishes for the New Year to you and your sister."

She snapped the ties on her reticule closed. "Happy Christmas, Miss Helmes. Miss Wellesley." Then Mrs. Cabot walked out the door.

Agatha hurried over to close the door before more heat escaped.

"I am shocked. Shocked!" Aunt Sally finally said with a decided lack of emotion. "If she thinks four people are a lot to cook for, what does she expect when she reaches London?"

"More pay for more meals? Aunt Sally, have you ever—?"

"No, and I think I shall never again."

"You realize she's left us with nothing for lunch?"

"Or tea or dinner," said her step-aunt, concerned with every meal of the day. "We were lucky to get breakfast."

"Shall we offer Mrs. Carter the job?"

"Do you think she would take it?"

A knock fell on the door, then it opened. The Vicar Rampling stuck his head into the room. "Ladies, am I intruding? Mrs. Cabot said to let myself in."

Aunt Sally gathered up her skirts. "No, Delilah, go back to the study. Agatha, I am going to speak with Mrs. Carter. Please excuse me, Rev. Rampling." And she headed for the kitchen and its door to the potager garden with the quickest route to the steward's cottage.

Agatha hid her sigh at her aunt's abandonment. She offered a calm façade to the vicar as he advanced to shake hands. Then she led him into the drawing room.

After sweeping Aunt Sally's paper chains to the floor, the Rev. Rampling commandeered the long sofa. Agatha raised her eyebrows then positioned herself near the fire. "I regret that I have no tea to offer you, sir. Mrs. Cabot just tendered her notice."

"Ah, yes, she said as much to me."

"She is off to London, to her sister, where she will cook for her sister's boarders."

He planted his hands on his knees. "I was not aware—ah, that she had decided upon this course."

"Nor were we, I assure you. She said that she had set forward these plans with her sister in October! Can you imagine? You find Aunt Sally and me quite flummoxed. Mrs. Cabot gave us no hint of any dissatisfaction."

"Ah, dissatisfaction. It creeps upon us quite unaware until we are against a brick wall and must take action."

The little homily sounded prepared. "Were you aware of Mrs. Cabot's dissatisfaction?"

"She mentioned something of that tenor, ah, about two weeks ago."

"She should have spoken to me, as her employer. She has been with us for several years, since before my stepfather's riding accident. I admit to expecting a little loyalty."

"I believe she was surprised, ah, by Mr. O'Malley's abrupt dismissal. Ah, many of us were so surprised. Your cousin wrote to me—."

"My cousin? My cousin Richard Helmes? In Ipswich?"

"Yes, that is his location. We often correspond—."

"You correspond with my cousin—about me?"

"Ah, he is interested in watching over you and feels that you never inform—."

"Spying on me," she muttered.

"Spying? Oh, no. Ah, he knows you are a woman alone. His business keeps him from visiting as he would like—."

"He enlists you to check up on me."

"To ensure your safety," he hastened to say.

"But he recommended that lecher O'Malley to me."

"A slander of Mr. O'Malley—."

She could no longer stand still. She paced away. Delilah ducked from under a side chair and prowled behind Agatha. "I do not slander Mr. O'Malley." She slewed around and came back. "Please, I interrupted. What did my cousin say in his letter to you?"

"He had learned of Mr. O'Malley's dismissal. Ah, he wanted to know of the reason."

The vicar fumbled inside his coat and produced a folded letter. As Agatha steamed, he opened the single sheet and skimmed the page. She wanted to snatch the letter away, but she clenched her hands at her sides and waited.

"Here. He writes, *Since I recommended the man, I would wish to know the reason for his dismissal. I cannot believe my faith was so misplaced.*"

"Well, it was. You can write that back to him."

"He does hold you in great esteem, Miss Helmes." The man looked up with an earnestness that looked simple rather than devious. "Listen. *I am my dear cousin's closest male relative. Even days and miles away from Helmes Farm, I stand somewhat in the position of her protector. The day that she and I are joined together—.*"

She stopped pacing and whirled around. "What?"

"Um, ah, um."

"The day we are *joined together*? My cousin is suggesting that we will marry?"

"An understanding of many years," he fumbled.

"*Not* an understanding on my part, sir." She loomed over him. Her fingers resembled claws, but she didn't snatch the letter away and fling it into the fire as she wanted to. Delilah hissed and arched her back. The vicar, having felt the cat's claws before, shrank back and twisted his legs away.

"If I have mistaken the matter—."

"Not your mistake, vicar, but my cousin's." She took a deep breath, trying to calm herself. "Cousin Richard tried to plant a finger on me and Helmes Farm before, but my stepfather routed him. He may think to marry me, but I have never and will never marry him. I don't love him." The plain words thudded out.

Her little speech didn't impress Rev. Rampling. "Ah, um, Mr. Helmes does not write of love but of companionship and security. Many a marriage is formed on that basis, and the partners are content together as they age. Women do marry men that they don't love."

"They do not marry men whom they cannot respect, not by choice, and I do not respect my cousin Richard. Is that the only reason for your visit? To check on me so you may send information to my cousin?"

"Well, ah, you have not attended services since Mr. O'Malley's dismissal."

"We have been busy here. I have a new steward."

"Ah, that would be the reason I saw a freight wagon at the cottage with boxes being carried inside."

"Yes. Please, do inform my cousin that he need not send a replacement steward. Or find a new cook. I believe we have a cook as well."

"But if Mrs. Cabot just left—."

"Yes, God provides in mysterious ways, before even we know our needs." Agatha could not prevent that sarcastic tone even as she realized the words were true.

"You need not be sacrilegious, Miss Helmes."

"Was I?" she asked, sugary sweet. "You need not be sanctimonious, Rev. Rampling. Do you have any other questions of me? Which you may convey in your very informative letter to my cousin."

"Ah, as to Mr. O'Malley's dismissal."

"You *are* in my cousin's pocket, aren't you? You'd best climb out. He has—." She stopped. No, she would not reveal what Jess had said, and the two puzzle pieces that slid together to explain her cousin's mysterious increase in funds. "Your focus is to be in this village. Lord Chalmesley would not wish to hear this living had fallen to a man who meddled beyond his parish."

"Miss Helmes—."

"You may inform my cousin that Mr. O'Malley was terminated from his position when he accosted me, here in this house. Now, I think we have had a full morning. Good day to you, Reverend."

She had left him with no recourse but retreat. He went, babbling the usual parting platitudes. In the seconds before she closed the door, he finally heard the word *accosted*. She thankfully closed the door on his fish-gasping mouth. His few words had given her several worries.

"The best thing I can say for that man," Aunt Sally commented from behind her, "he's timely. He knows when it is time for him to leave."

Agatha managed a small smile even as thoughts swirled and swirled. "He's in league with Cousin Richard, keeping a watchful eye on us, because Richard has suggested he and I will someday marry."

Her step-aunt's jaw dropped.

"I see you are as shocked as I am. I disabused the reverend of the notion that a marriage between Richard and me will ever occur."

"To believe that—. Has he *ever* met your cousin?"

"They correspond regularly, he tells me."

"That man's an idiot. Even my cats think so."

"Yes, Samson and Delilah do understand who's to be trusted in this world. Did you see Mrs. Carter?"

"I did. She is delighted with the offer, but she doesn't quite know how to manage breakfasts here and at the cottage. I have assured her we'll work something out, after Boxing Day."

Agatha hugged her aunt. "I knew you would work it out. Did you happen to mention that nothing's prepared for tonight's supper?"

Chapter 5 ~ Friday to Saturday, 27 & 28 December

Jess woke coughing.

The blackness of night enveloped him. He lay still until another cough wracked him. He wasn't ill. What was wrong?

Then he heard his mother coughing in the room across the landing. He threw back the bedcovers. When his bare feet hit the floor, the boards felt hot.

And he heard a muted roar, a crackling that could only be fire.

He snatched on his trousers and shoved his feet into his boots. A second thought had him grab up his wallet and stuff that into his boot as well.

The door felt as hot as the floorboards. He didn't hear his mother coughing. He jerked open the door.

The upper landing had a shifting amber glow. Glass crashed downstairs. Jess peered over the banister. He didn't see flames, but flickering shadows climbed the wall of the stairwell. The high ceilings below had probably kept the flames from feeding on that fuel, but the roar warned him that the house would soon burst from the increasing heat. He thought he heard shouts, but the fire covered them.

They had no chance of getting out by the stairs, but a rose trellis climbed the brick wall just outside his mother's window.

He went in, slamming the door behind him. His mother didn't wake. The smoke seemed thicker here, the floors hotter. He shook her hard, harder.

"Jess?" Her slurred voice sounded drunk on the smoke. "Jess, what is it?"

"Fire. Throw some clothes on, Ma."

"Fire?" The word roused her as little else could have. Every cottager's fear was fire, especially when it funneled up the stairs to the thatch roofs. The steward's cottage had thin slate, but the boards under the slate would burn just as fast as a cottage did.

He opened the window. Cold air gushed in as hot smoke rushed out. Jess inhaled the cooler air, hoping it would clear his head and lungs. He heard his mother moving behind him.

The flames lit the ground around the cottage. His mother's room was above the kitchen, but no light came out that window. He remembered shutting the kitchen door before he climbed the stairs, a last deed after the checking the windows and doors. He'd felt a sense of pride in getting moved into the cottage.

And now it burned.

The trellis came right to the window casement. He gave the wood cross-support a hard shake. It seemed sturdy enough. It would have to be.

He crossed to her other window, the dormered one above the little dining room. The dancing light told that the fire burned in the front rooms. He could see people standing in the little lane beyond the gate.

"Get out!" someone shouted when they saw him. "The whole ground floor is on fire! Hurry!"

"Can we go out by the stairs?" his mother asked.

"They're on fire." He took her purse and shoved it into the pocket of her coat, the capacious one he had outgrown several years before and which she had refused to give up. "You first, Ma."

She glanced at the open window. "Jess, you need a shirt and a coat."

He opened the door. The heat blasted him. Greedy flames licked at the stair steps, rushing to climb up. More crashes came from below. He slammed it shut.

"All our things," she cried.

"Come on, Ma."

He helped her climb through the window. One hand gripped her left arm and the other steadied her shoulder as she started down the trellis. When she was below his help, he noticed how the wood shook with her weight. He dared not start down while she was on it—but her progress was slow, too slow. He knew better than to hurry her.

She was only half-way down. To keep from saying the words that would only slow her more, Jess glanced back at the door. The crack under it revealed brighter light. The fire was advancing. The night breeze chilled his slick skin. He couldn't figure out why he was sweating when he was cold with fear.

She was close to the ground. Flames burst through the back window of the steward's office.

"Jump, Ma!"

She glanced up. Then she looked down and obeyed.

Someone had run around from the front. When she landed, he lunged forward and dragged her up and away from the house. And Jess climbed out.

At the first sag of the wooden support, he didn't think it would take his weight, but he had no other options. The flames were licking under the chamber door. Another cross-support broke under his boot and he slid down, saved only by his hands ripping down the main post. He planted his boots closer to the vertical supports and went faster.

Flames burst through his back window. A woman screamed—but that was behind him, in the garden and safe.

More frames broke. He slid, grabbing at supports. He caught, looked to see how far he'd fallen, then jumped the rest of the way.

The frozen ground jarred through him. He collapsed to his knees. Then he scrambled up and limped away.

And the kitchen window blew out.

He ducked to avoid the shards. They missed him. He hadn't taken two more steps before his mother was on him. "Are you hurt? Where are you hurt?"

His hands ached. His feet and ankles felt shattered. But he put an arm around her shoulders. "Nothing that matters. You still got your purse?" When she nodded, he pulled out his wallet. "Put this in your other pocket."

She shoved it deep then tucked her hands in her sleeves. He urged her forward by the means of his embracing arm and herded her to the front of the house.

A ragged cheer sounded when they were spotted. The number of watching people surprised Jess. Buckets were at the feet of some, empty he noticed. Three women prised his mother away from him, and he looked back at the cottage he'd felt proud to move into. Flames leaped in every window.

"Anyone know what happened?"

"Burning when we got here," a man said.

"Who spotted it?"

"Ol' Denny."

"Where is he?"

"Right here, steward." The old man shouldered through the crowd. "No stoppin' it, was there?"

"What did you see?"

"Flames through the windows. Banged on the doors front and back. It couldn't get either of them opened."

"They were on a simple latch."

"That so? They didn't budge when I put my shoulder to 'em. I got old shoulders, though. When we got back with buckets, the fire was in all the windows downstairs."

"It spread fast then."

The old man gave Jess a direct look. "M'own thoughts."

*Set then.* Yet Jess kept his suspicions unsaid. He had no way to confirm them. "Has anyone alerted the main house?"

From the back a man said, "Tassie went."

"Here they come," another said and pointed.

Agatha Helmes came at a run, a dark coat flying behind her. She had flung the heavy coat over her night rail, but she hadn't buttoned it. She wore gardening boots, probably one of the pairs that stayed in the back entryway. The scrawny woman hurrying behind was probably Tassie.

As she reached the crowd, Agatha slowed. She bethought herself of her thin night rail and dragged the coat closed. Her hair was slipping its braid. The firelight gave amber to her skin, and Jess reckoned he had inhaled too much smoke because he thought she looked lovely. She said something to a woman when she reached the crowd. Tassie grabbed a third woman then started back to the house.

The people parted to let her through. Her gaze skittered over Jess and his chilled flesh then searched and found his mother. She angled toward his mother. "Mrs. Carter, are you hurt? Are either of you hurt?" She looked back at Jess then, as if she dared not look too long at him, she cast a look over the crowd. "Is anyone hurt?"

"No, Miss" and "No, m'm" came as scattered answers.

She slipped an arm about Jess' mother's waist. "You're not hurt?" she asked again.

"Jess' hands—."

Agatha finally let her eyes light on him for longer than a second. He turned his hands over, and other people joined her gasp at the black blood smearing his palms.

"I'm scratched some," he allowed.

"Not burned?"

"No, this is from the trellis. It broke with my weight."

"And you, Mrs. Carter?"

"Jess got me out first."

She hugged the woman. "God be thanked."

"Aye, for I almost didn't wake up. Ma was out of it. I had a hard time waking her." He glanced back at the cottage and realized death had brushed close by.

"All our things," his mother cried.

Agatha put both arms around his mother. "Things can be replaced. Lives cannot."

Over his mother's white head, she met Jess' eyes. And she surprised him then: She didn't ask how the fire started, nor did she speculate on what its cause would have been.

When his mother's tears stopped, Agatha released one arm to face the crowd. "Aunt Sally has hot tea, and Tassie will have rounded up some bread and cold meat for sandwiches, thanks to Mrs. Carter's cooking yesterday. Please go up and get what you need. When this burns out, we'll decide what to do."

The crowd dispersed. His mother hesitated. Agatha lifted a hand, and a woman stepped forward to link arms with his mother and urge her on to the house.

And then only Agatha and Jess and Denny remained before the burning cottage.

Arms folded, Agatha watched the fire. The flames licked out of all the windows and nibbled at portions of the roof. "Who saw it first?"

"Me, Miss."

She didn't even glance at Denny. "Did you notice anything?"

"A line of fire in all the rooms downstairs. Doors wedged shut front and back."

"Wedged shut?"

"I couldn't budge `em. I may be old, but I got strong shoulders still."

"Yes." Her gaze flicked to Jess.

"Anything we had to steal was in our rooms with us. We got that out, at least."

She nodded, understanding him, but she turned back to the old man. "You didn't break a window to get in and stop it, Denny."

"Thought I could get back with people and buckets. Not fast enough, I reckon."

"Not if the fire was following a path set out for it," Jess put in. He hadn't missed Denny's description, even if she had.

"Lamp oil, you reckon, Miss?"

"What else could it be, Denny?"

"Ayuh."

Fire climbed over the roof, and slate pieces began sliding off, to crash and break on the frozen ground.

"A dangerous enemy," Agatha said.

Jess realized that Agatha Helmes had missed nothing. She tracked her own thought process, and while he had parts of it, she had other pieces that he had not even considered.

"O'Malley ain't quit the district," the old man allowed.

"But no evidence," she countered.

"Wait up," Jess said. Their conversation was running faster than he'd expected. Yet it tracked along lines he had suspected as soon as he woke up coughing. As Agatha said, all their speculations had no evidence. He chafed his chilling skin and wondered how he and his mother had managed to wake up. "You think someone set the fire, to get back at me, and you think that was O'Malley."

"A straight line to `em," Denny said.

"We have no evidence," Agatha repeated. She re-wrapped her coat around her then wrapped her arms around her front. "It is curious that the fire occurs your first night in the cottage, Jess. Some might lay it to carelessness, but neither you nor your mother are that careless. Or do you doubt Denny's eyes? And his strong shoulders? He is an *old* man."

"*Hrmph*. Not that old. M'eyes don't lie. I know what I saw."

"Incontrovertible. But not enough to stand in court. Not enough to counter the gossip O'Malley's supporters will have swirling around. Certainly not enough to prevent my cousin from horning in, claiming O'Malley is of good reputation."

"He still pokin' his fingers in?" Denny asked while Jess winced inwardly. At least Dick Helmes' letter of introduction burned up with the cottage.

"He and the vicar correspond regularly, if you can believe it."

"Oh, I ken. That vicar's an idiot."

"We're straying from the point," Jess interrupted to get them back on track and away from Dick Helmes. "We're standing out here freezing because we can't have this conversation around anyone else? Is that it? You both think someone set this fire deliberately. Did you see anyone standing back from the house, watching?"

"No, but I weren't lookin'. Once I spotted the fire and shouted at you, whoever might have been watchin' would have kept well hidden. Teller's dog was barkin', though. Something stirred him up. It won't bark at foxes."

Inside the house something crashed down. The flames guttered then flared brighter. Sparks gushed into the air and drifted into the night sky.

"We got no evidence," Denny said and spat.

Agatha pushed a fist against her lips then shook her head. "You're right, Denny. We have nothing. I will notify Lord Chalmesley tomorrow—or rather today. I will tell him that we think this is arson but have no proof. He will likely send a constable to poke around a bit."

Jess stared at her. Her hair was wild, blown by the wind. Her face was pinched with cold. Her mouth was primmed with anger. And he wanted to pull her into his arms and thank God that he'd been given more days to be with her. "Then what?"

"And then nothing, as that is the way when we have no evidence. I could have run O'Malley off months ago if those girls would have testified that he took advantage of them, but not a one of them would."

"Scared. Ashamed. Both," Denny opined.

"If he wants me dead, we can't just let him run loose. He burned the cottage with me and my ma in it."

"We must do nothing—until we have evidence, of whatever sort we can find. What else can we do, Jess? Shall I weep thousands of tears? Snatch my hair out? Scream? You missed that. I was still at the house then. Aunt Sally had to calm me down."

"You got an acid tongue, Miss. He's got a right to worry. An' he an' his ma are homeless, even more now than when they arrived."

"I apologize. I'm—."

"Hush." Jess draped an arm around her shoulders. Now that he knew how she'd reacted and that she hadn't just watched dispassionately, he strangely felt better about the fire and their narrow escape and the loss of all their worldly goods. "What now?"

"Now?"

"You can't stay out here all night watching the fire burn out. It's too cold."

"I have a coat. You don't even have a shirt."

"I'll watch," Denny offered. "Teller's on his way back. He can spell me. It'll burn out by dawn or thereabouts, with hot spots here an' there. You two go on up to the house."

His ma waited with a shirt they'd found somewhere. Jess washed off the soot and dirt and sweat, washed the smoke out of his hair, then sat at the kitchen table with Delilah on his knee and Samson draped over a boot and drank coffee till dawn.

Neither he nor Agatha shared their suspicions with his mother and her step-aunt.

Miss Wellesley looked her questions, but Agatha shrugged, and the moment passed. She had changed into a drab wool dress and scraped her hair back, although little tendrils escaped that rigid control and curled around her face.

Sunrise found Jess standing before the ruins of the cottage.

The front wall had collapsed. The chimneys on either end still stood. Most of the back wall remained. The bones of the stairs climbed to nothing. Charred timbers lay at angles where they'd crashed down.

"When I was a girl, I always thought this was the prettiest cottage, with its rose trellises. In spring and summer the bees buzzed around the roses constantly. They were overgrown and needed judicious pruning. Your mother had spoken of bringing the garden back. I had hoped to see that."

"We can transplant the roses. Ma will know when and how."

"Good. Beauty can still come from these ashes. Isn't that in the Bible somewhere?" She turned. "I can't look at it, not yet. I get angry."

"You truly think it was O'Malley?"

"He is the only one that makes the most sense. He has a grudge against you and me. But his lordship's constable will want evidence, not theory. Come back to the house, Jess. Aunt Sally has found more clothes for you, if you don't mind cast-offs."

He looked at the linen shirt and woolen jacket with its leather collar and cuffs. "How could I mind cast-offs of this quality?"

"They were my stepfather's before he lost the use of his legs. A riding accident crippled him the last three years of his life. They are not truly a dead man's clothes."

"I'm too practical to worry about that. Your stepfather, that's Miss Wellesley's brother, isn't it?" He turned with her toward the house. Even in her woolen gown and dark coat, she matched his stride without trouble. He liked that about her, a woman who matched him rather than a woman who followed or claimed to a false weakness and cried for help. "Did your step-aunt live with you before then?"

"She came when my mother died. She didn't have the two cats then, only Samson's mother. Delilah is a recent acquisition, cast out when the vicar came to his new living."

"And that earned him Aunt Sally's undying enmity for not liking cats?"

"Exactly." Her face lit up with humor, and she shared the story of the vicar's first visit, when Delilah made her distaste for the man quite known.

Until she smiled, Jess hadn't noticed how pale she looked, with dark shadows under her eyes. The burned cottage was worrying her more than she was willing to share.

Chapter 6 ~ Tuesday, 31 December

The bonfire was bigger than in previous years. The village children ran about with little sparklers. Young couples slipped away from the fire, seeking the darkness that lovers craved.

Mrs. Carter had cried off, pleading that the celebration was too soon after the house fire.

Aunt Sally had gone home complaining of the cold.

Agatha had stayed, hoping for—what? She felt foolish, but she still couldn't get the image of a shirtless Jess Carter out of her mind. Since Tuesday she'd spent much too much time remembering his broad shoulders, defined abdominal muscles, and breeches sagging below his waist. Stanton Myers had had the same height but a leaner build, and their hasty coupling in secret hadn't given her any opportunity to study the male form. Jess Carter's male form was worthy of study.

The bonfire's glow hid her flushed cheeks. She pressed her knuckles to her mouth and looked around for the hundredth time, looking for her new steward. Then she looked away and chatted with some of the villagers.

She had to cast that night's image from her mind. She needed to return to the house. Yet she lingered, waiting with the villagers for the church bells to toll the New Year.

As the doctor's wife described her child's latest escapade at the mill pond, Agatha peeked around. Yes, Jess was still there. He was talking with Denny and a few men who worked the farm. His height identified him, just as it did her. He hadn't offered to come near her, not since that first day, when he'd caught her after that foolish swoon and held her on his lap. He kept a respectable distance. Was that because he'd become her employee or because she didn't attract him?

She'd had only a couple of beaux, and one of those had abandoned her. A long Meg, she'd heard one man tell his fellows, with nothing but long limbs to commend her. Stanton had certainly had no reason to remain once he'd breached her defenses and had her vow of undying love.

All he had of her now was her grief over the baby he'd given her and she'd lost in birth, the tiny boy who slept in the cold ground.

She glanced at the church. Candles in the windows and a lamp in the belfry lit the church for the festivities. The church yard to the side wasn't lit, but enough light spilled over from the bonfire to see a way through the graves. No matter how much light, she could find the little grave in absolute dark. She had haunted the little mound for the first couple of years. It marked the loss of her dreams. Aunt Sally had told her, once, that she had feared Agatha would go mad, what with her night-time wanderings and daily distraction and smothering sadness.

She had climbed out of that hole, though. She didn't intend to dig another one.

But she hadn't visited the grave since November. Excusing herself, she crossed the common green and angled for the cemetery.

The Helmes obelisk marked five generations of the line, ending with her father. Her mother had chosen a place with the Wellesleys. Robbie Wellesley lay beside Agatha's mother, guarding her in death as he'd once guarded her in life. Agatha knelt and pressed a gloved hand to her mother's stone and then to her stepfather's. A little farther on, in a corner of the Helmes plot, was a little lamb with no more than a name carved on its base. Robert Helmes, her little lost lamb.

She knelt, feeling the cold ground seep into her knees, and used her hand to sweep dead leaves and twigs from the little grave. Nine years ago. He would have been the age that Little Mike was now. He'd never opened his eyes.

The celebration continued. Talk and laughter, a child shouting.

Her grief welled up, catching her by surprise. Why now? She bent her head and tried to master it, talking harshly to herself. It was self-pity, choked dreams that she wouldn't admit. It was hopelessness when she had a good life, a more comfortable life than many who came through Helmesford. It was defeatism when she worked hard to remain cheerful. She wouldn't be dragged into that morass of depression again.

She was shivering hard when a voice jerked her out of the personal darkness. "Your aunt said you might come here."

Agatha visited a blessing and a curse on Aunt Sally. Her step-aunt knew her too well. Stiff from the cold, she climbed to her feet. Jess' hard fingers gripped her arm to help her then fell away. Without looking around, she asked, "What did she tell you?"

"About your drunkard father. Your crippled stepfather. Your son born out of wedlock."

She couldn't read his voice, and the darkness would hide his expression. "Are you not shocked?"

"People make mistakes. The both of us did. I fell in with smugglers. You fell in love." When she didn't respond, he added, "When did the babe die? Was it at the New Year?"

"It was no date so remarkable. Just a day in July."

"The father?"

"He left many months before."

"More fool he."

She wanted to see his face then. She did look, but they were too far from the bonfire to see features clearly. The darkness hid him effectively, as it must hide her. "You should return to your friends."

"Denny headed back a while ago. We should head back as well."

He took her arm again. She let him guide her to the low wall that marked the cemetery's environs. He scooped her into his arms, lifting her as if she were as light as thistledown. Agatha squeaked and gripped his shoulders. She caught his flash of grin, his teeth white in his face.

And she marveled, for with a little talk and a simple action, he'd lifted her out of the grieving past.

Jess lowered her to the other side of the wall and climbed over himself. He took her hand and headed for the road that led to the farm.

"Do you not want to wait for the bell-ringing?" Agatha asked. "You shouldn't miss it. The pub will open briefly, so everyone can toast the New Year."

"It's colder than a witch's—well, it's colder than I like to be out in. You're shivering, too. We can toast the New Year sitting in front of the kitchen range my mother's enamored of, with hot cider heated by a bit of whiskey. That'll do me. I have to be up early."

"It's the New Year. We can sleep in a little."

He looked her way, and she saw the flash of his teeth as he grinned. "Your new steward is shocked by that suggestion." Then the grin vanished. "Did you hear from his lordship?"

"Not yet. I do not expect him to reply, not by letter. His constable will come soon, if he comes at all. Lord Chalmesley may not think there is anything worth investigating."

Jess grunted. They walked in silence. Agatha counted through several things to say, but everything sounded artificial.

The bonfire was long out of view when the church bells started ringing through the changes. They stopped and looked back toward the village. The light in the belfry flickered as the four bells rang in sequence.

"Do they—," he started then said, "Ah," as the little bell held up to let the others ring together. As the changes rang out again, he looked across at Agatha. "Happy New Year, Agatha Helmes."

"Happy New Year, Jess Carter." She sensed him hesitating. "Yes?" she prompted.

He huffed a laugh. "You'll think me forward, but may I kiss you? A kiss for good fortune in the New Year."

Her heart jumped up and down, her emotions like an excited little girl. "A kiss for good fortune," she repeated. "Yes, of course." She lifted her mouth for a simple salutation, brief and platonic.

He slipped a hand to her nape and drew her two steps closer. He leaned in, hesitated, then set his mouth to hers. It began platonic, a simple pressing of their lips, then his tongue touched the seam of her mouth. Her mouth opened in surprise, and he delved inside.

When he lifted his head, Agatha was clinging to him to keep upright. He rested his forehead against hers. At some point he had wrapped his other arm around her and dragged her close. Even through her heavy coat, she could feel his heat.

"Happy New Year, Agatha," he repeated.

"Happy New Year, Jess."

Someone hooted behind them. He set her away from him and turned to meet the youth running up. Others came behind.

Her cheeks flaming and her lips still tingling, Agatha greeted them with a calmness at odds with the riot in her blood. She let the noise of good humor swirl around her. They had left the village well in advance of everyone, and now everyone surrounded them. Had she gotten so lost in his kisses?

No one remarked on how close they had been standing when Georgie called out to Jess. No one could see her heightened color. No one commented when Jess took her hand and placed it in the crook of his arm. The walk back to the farm passed in a blur. People called good wishes as they separated from the mass to turn to their homes.

They reached the house. Jess held the door for her. Someone had left two lamps for them in the entrance hall. He dropped the latch to lock it then gripped her arm.

*Is he going to kiss me again?* Agatha's heart started pounding.

He slipped his hand down to squeeze hers. "I'll check the doors and windows before I turn in. Goodnight, Agatha."

Her foolish heart paused then started erratically. "Good night."

As she lay in her cold bed, she wondered if God were offering another opportunity or another temptation.

In the days that followed, she realized that she was offered neither. Jess once more kept his distance. Indeed, he seemed to find ways to avoid her except when she gave him directions for the day.

In the nights that followed, she stared into the darkness and refused to cry.

.~.~.~.

# 1812

Wednesday, 5 February

"I'm Constable Evans, Miss Helmes. His lordship sent me." The slim man with sharp features removed his gloves then held out his hand.

Agatha controlled the lift of her eyebrows. She shook the man's hand. He had a firm clasp and cool skin with a few callouses that were at odds with his neat, dark suit. She led him to her study and motioned to the chair before her desk. "You are much delayed, Constable. I notified his lordship over a month ago."

"We had another matter before us." He took the offered chair but didn't lean back. His curiously lichen green eyes pinned her. "I noticed that the cottage ruins have not been cleared."

"You've been there?" She planted herself and folded her hands in her lap.

"I rode in from the village this morning. I've been there since I arrived."

"No one noticed you?" That worried her.

"It is a cold morning, Miss Helmes. I imagine most people are doing what farm chores they can inside. I did meet your steward Mr. Carter."

"I am gratified that not everyone let you pass by."

"He said he and his mother were in the cottage asleep when the fire began."

"As I informed his lordship in my letter."

"I have also spoken with the old man Mr. Denny. His testimony is most singular. But he seems a steady witness."

"He is most steady, sir. We all depend on Denny. His mind is very sharp."

"I gathered that. His witness never varied, no matter how I approached it." His stoic expression broke. "I like that man. He reminds me of my grandfather. But that is a personal comment, Miss, and not related to my investigation. Neither Mr. Carter nor Mr. Denny would name a person they suspected, but I understand you had recently fired a steward."

*Tread carefully.* "Yes. Reece O'Malley."

He took a little notebook and pencil from his coat pocket. Flipping it open, he looked up at her. "Would you spell his name, please?" He printed block letters then looked up. "Do you suspect Mr. O'Malley?"

"Denny did say, on the night of the fire, that Mr. O'Malley had been sighted in the village. He was angry at his dismissal. I will not speculate on more, Constable."

He nodded once. He flipped back a page then returned. "Would you tell me what occasioned the termination of his employment with you? I understand he had been here several months. That would suggest

his work was acceptable."

"His work was minimally acceptable. His predecessors were wholly unacceptable. I likely would have retained Mr. O'Malley as steward if he had not accosted me in this very room."

The clouds moved away from the sun. Light poured into the study. A shaft of it struck his face. His pupils shrank to pinpoints. He winced and shifted a little, tilting his head to protect his eyes. The sunlight fell on his hair, turning it from lackluster to golden halo. "He accosted you? In what way?"

Her eyebrows rose sky-high. "Are such details necessary?"

"I believe so, Miss Helmes."

She narrowed her eyes. "I would prefer this information not be bandied about, Constable. I have a reputation to maintain."

"I understand. The details of his termination need not be dwelled upon in court, should a case against him result from my investigation. The details, please?"

She flushed as she recounted the barest information. "He grabbed me. He dragged me across this desk and broke my grandfather's silver inkwell. He tried to stick his tongue in my mouth. He was trying to throttle me when Mr. Carter intervened."

"This is the Mr. Carter who is now your steward?"

"Yes."

"What did Mr. Carter do to intervene?"

"He shoved him off me and then knocked him down. I do not know how many blows they exchanged. When Mr. O'Malley remained on the floor, cursing at me and Mr. Carter, I terminated his employment there and then. Before the sun set, Mr. Carter passed on to him the remainder of his wage. He had to vacate the steward's cottage, but I understand that he did not leave it until the morning."

"You did not see to his removal yourself?"

"I did not want to set eyes on him again."

"I see. But he remained in the village."

"I banished him from my property, Constable. After losing his employment, I would have expected him to leave. He did not. Only Lord Chalmesley can ban him from the district."

"You did not request that of his lordship?"

Clouds covered the sun again. Constable Evans returned to ordinary, and Agatha marveled at the change even as she answered. "I did not. I was embarrassed by the circumstances. I saw no reason to tell the whole world."

"His lordship is not the whole world." She could only shrug. His mouth compressed. "And how was it that Mr. Carter was present when Mr. O'Malley accosted you?"

"He was waiting in the hall. He was seeking employment. He heard—things when Mr. O'Malley put his hands on me. He must tell you those details. We have discussed what brought him into the room. I was only glad that he appeared when he did. I thanked God for his timely arrival."

The constable flicked back several pages, read silently over several, then returned to the page he filled out based on her words. "Were there any injuries from this assault?"

"I bit his tongue."

His eyes widened. "Desperate measures, Miss Helmes."

She looked back steadily. "I was desperate, Constable. Mr. Carter came in at that point and kept Mr. O'Malley from strangling me. He was angry enough that I feared for my life."

He wrote a few lines, flipped to a new page, then looked up. "One would think, Miss Helmes, that Mr. O'Malley would focus any retaliation upon you as opposed to Mr. Carter?"

"I cannot answer for the workings of his mind. This is the chief reason that I did not voice my suspicions to his lordship. They are without foundation, Constable. I have also never said our arsonist is logical, just wicked."

"Yes. I understand that distinction."

He stared at the empty page, and she wondered what he considered. His next questions? The validity of her answers? O'Malley's guilt? For having a remarkably mobile face, he could shield his thoughts completely.

"You said that you've been to the cottage?" She broke the silence before it stretched her nerves too far.

"No one else has been through the place?"

"No. Everyone has kept well back, including the children. Although I am certain several small boys were tempted at the prospect of getting very dirty."

Evans cracked a smile then immediately removed it. "Yes. Mr. Denny was kind enough to let me change in his cottage."

"Then you have searched through the ashes."

"A cursory search. I will conduct a more detailed one tomorrow. Tell me, Miss Helmes, has the steward's cottage always been tenanted?"

"No. For many years it sat vacant. My stepfather appointed men to keep it in repair. Before this past year, when it housed our successive stewards, it had not been habited for ten years."

"Would you by chance remember who last lived there?"

"His name was Stanton Myers."

"Was, Miss Helmes?"

"He may still call himself Stanton Myers. He may call himself something else now. He left here in a bit of a hurry. I have neither seen nor heard from him since."

"And the occasion of his leaving?"

"I was four months gone with his child," she said baldly, her color high, "and he had expressed no desire to marry me. My stepfather was displeased when I informed him. Stanton—he had left by then."

"I see. And before Mr. Myers?"

"Before him?" She frowned. What was the purpose of these questions? "That would be my father's last steward, Graeme MacDonald. He died a few years after my father. We let him live retired in the cottage."

"Where is he buried?"

Her frown increased. "In the village cemetery."

"This was a public burial?"

"Very public. Old Mac was well liked."

"Then it was not his bones that I found in the cottage."

Ice filled her. "You found—someone's bones?" Her voice sounded far away. Black edged her vision.

"Yes, Miss Helmes. Beneath the stair. Walled in, perhaps, into what must have been a storage area."

"Walled in beneath the stairs?"

She didn't hear anymore. She slid from the chair as the blackness overwhelmed her.

Chapter 7 ~ Wednesday, 5 February

"Didn't you see her look faint?" Jess snapped.

Agatha's breathing changed, and he realized she was back. He slipped an arm beneath her shoulders and lifted her a little. "Agatha, drink this."

She murmured something, but when he held the glass to her lips, she drank. Then she sputtered and coughed. The whiskey and the coughing brought bright color to her cheeks. He dared to lift her more and cradle her against his chest. He touched the glass to her lips again.

She sipped obediently then turned her face away as she breathed through the burn. "Did I swoon this time?"

"Still just a here and there and back again. I was waiting in the hall."

"Are we—doomed to repeat that first meeting?"

"I wouldn't say doomed."

She was shivering now. He set the glass aside and chafed her left arm. Her right arm was trapped against him. He wished he could put her on his lap, but that constable hovered behind him, with bright eyes watching everything and thinking dozens of things, none good, Jess would warrant. He already looked at Jess askance because he'd cradled Agatha in his arms before he lifted her from the floor. He had carried her to the window bench again. And then he'd used her first name. The damned constable was likely thinking they were lovers.

Jess wished they were.

He shoved the thought away and tried to get her to drink more whiskey.

"No." She turned away again. She squirmed a little and tried to sit up. He held her tight.

The constable intruded again. "If Miss Helmes can answer a few more questions."

"She's barely got her eyes open," he growled.

The man stepped back.

"Hush, Jess," she murmured. "It's better to answer everything now. Let me sit up, please."

He propped her up, worried when she swayed, but she put both hands on the edge of the bench to steady herself. He added the strong support of his body on her left.

Agatha lifted her gaze to the constable. "Ask away, sir."

"We were talking about the skeleton I found, Miss Helmes. The framing of the staircase protected the corpse from falling beams."

She shut her eyes as if pained. Jess worried and slid an arm around her.

"I remember." She opened her eyes. "Beneath the stairs."

"Yes. The fire burned away his clothing and similar superficial identifiers. I do know he was murdered. And I found this on his hand." He held out a ring, large and heavy.

She stared at the charred ring. Jess felt the reluctance in her stiffened body. Yet when the constable continued to hold the ring out to her, she took it with a hand that shook. She turned it over before placing it in her opened palm. Fire had smoked the gold but not melted it. Jess couldn't see the emblem clearly, but it looked like a sword cutting through a barred knight's shield.

"This is Mr. Myers' ring." Agatha handed it back.

The constable didn't take it. "You are certain."

"I saw it many times. He said the eldest child of his family always received it." Her eyes finally lifted from the ring to bore into his. "It should be returned to his family, Constable Evans. Their direction is Warwickshire, the town of Wellesbourne Montford."

"Your child should not receive it, Miss Helmes?"

Jess felt her shivers begin, and he clamped her tighter to his side.

"My child did not—did not live, Constable," she said faintly. Then she straightened, trying to rely on no one, as she had done for years. Her voice firmed. "I believe Mr. Myers has a brother and two sisters. When he left—when I thought he had left—I did contact his family. They had not heard of his whereabouts and asked that I not contact them again."

"And you never did?"

"I acquiesced to their wishes, sir. His brother Greville Myers did come a month after my child's—passing. I did not speak with him. My stepfather did."

"You do not know what passed between them?"

She drew a deep breath and again handed over the ring. "I did not care to know. I still do not. My step-aunt may be able to relate their conversation to you."

Again he refused the ring. "Take it," Jess growled.

The constable started then accepted the ring. He dropped the ring into a little metal box then dropped that into his pocket. Then he clasped his hands behind his back. "From what you tell me, I would think that no one here held any grudge against Stanton Myers."

Agatha straightened her back from its tired sag. "I was shocked when he left. I am shocked to hear he was here, beneath that stairwell. You said you knew he was murdered. How do you know?"

"Bullet to the head," he said brutally.

She jerked. "No."

"Aye," Jess said. "I saw the skull after the constable had us dig him out."

"That's where you've been," she said faintly.

"Denny's there now, waiting on the casket from the village to put him in. Do you want him buried here? Near your little boy?"

He didn't think she was going to answer, then slowly the words came. "He should be buried at his home."

"We will need to retain the remains—."

"Then you can take 'em with you," Jess said sturdily. "They're not staying here."

The constable eyed him, and Jess met his gaze squarely. He had displeased the man. Well, the man displeased him. He hadn't cared that Agatha had fainted. He hadn't cared once that every question pained her.

"You are a great defender of Miss Helmes."

"Who else is going to defend her? I guess you're down to just one question. Did the arsonist not know burning the cottage would reveal the old murder, or did he burn it hoping to set everything crosswise here, with us having to answer questions about the old murder?"

"How would anyone know? Anyone other than the murderer, I mean?"

That brought Agatha's head up. Good. Jess didn't like her mired in the past.

"The murderer could have told him, or O'Malley could have found the remains poking around. When I carried our things in, I wondered why there was no storage beneath the stairs. I'd already told my ma about putting in an access. It was only a matter of time before the body was found."

"I believe, Mr. Carter," the constable pointed out with a smooth tongue, "that you have missed the more pressing question: Was Stanton Myers killed because he would not marry Miss Helmes, or because he would have married her? The first would be someone angry for her. Her stepfather, perhaps."

"No, not him," she protested. Jess tucked his arm closer, offering support. "I didn't tell him of my condition until after Stanton left."

"Then it's the second motive. Someone wanted to ensure she remain unmarried."

"Her cousin," Jess pointed out. He'd wanted to blame Dick Helmes for the last half-hour. Finally, he had his chance. He couldn't repeat Helmes' own words. He didn't want Agatha thinking he'd had a deal with the cousin she despised.

"My cousin Richard Helmes, in Ipswich," she supplied, and the constable dutifully recorded name and place. "He does think he has a right to the farm, Constable. Any husband of mine would ensure that my cousin claimed no rights."

"Does he have a right, Miss Helmes?"

"Not according to my father's will. And my grandfather's. And his father's. As far back as the Helmes have used wills. I believe they removed the inheritance from primogeniture to the legal will as a means to curry favor with Elizabeth the First. I would not be the first female to benefit from the will over the old male inheritance laws."

"I see."

"You need to look into her cousin," Jess pronounced, pushing the part. "O'Malley came here on the man's recommendation. That means they were working together. He kept an eye on the farm for her cousin."

Evans found the flaw. "But this O'Malley accosted Miss Helmes. Would that not negate any agreement with her cousin?"

"Maybe O'Malley thought to cut him out, once he realized the land was hers, no matter what her cousin said. You need to go to Ipswich and look into her cousin. Richard Helmes. He owns a warehouse on Austin Street."

Agatha had nodded through Jess' direction, and the constable added his information. But he shook his head. "While I do see two crimes have occurred, I cannot take action. I have no evidence, just circumstance, to lead me in the directions you are pointing."

"Circumstance is waving a red flag at this bull then," Jess grumbled, "because I believe it."

"You believe O'Malley is involved in the arson or Mr. Helmes is involved in the murder?"

"Both."

Evans shook his head. "We have no reason to think either. I admit the circumstances of the arson do glare. Mr. O'Malley could have torched the steward's cottage at any time, yet he waited until you moved in. That seems a specific retribution against you, Mr. Carter. What does he hold against you?"

"I knocked him down twice."

"And you took his job."

"Are you going to arrest Mr. O'Malley?" Agatha interjected.

The constable shook his head again. "I understand he has left the district."

"Perhaps if you'd come when it first happened," Jess groused.

"If I had come too soon, the ashes would not have cooled enough for me to discover the remains of Mr. Myers."

"Constable," Agatha picked at a loose thread on her skirt, "is there a specific reason you delayed coming here?"

The man craned his neck, as if his starched collar bothered him. "His lordship advised me to delay."

Jess swore. From Agatha's chilly tone, he reckoned she had sworn mutely. "And did his lordship have a reason to delay your coming to us?"

"Miss Helmes, I am not in his lordship's confidence. Nevertheless, it is murder I found in that cottage."

"And the arson?" she pressed.

"I will file a report, Miss Helmes, and send a notice that Reece O'Malley is a man we're interested in. I remind you: we have no evidence. Without evidence or a confession, his lordship will not justify any action I take. He is magistrate, as you know. His word is the determining factor."

Jess stood, looming without even approaching the man. "And the murder?"

"Without evidence or a confession ... ."

"Aye, that's what I thought. You didn't even need to come."

"Indeed, I did. No one else would have searched through the burnt-out cottage. I did find Mr. Myers' corpse."

Jess escorted the constable out, glad to shut the door on the man. He returned to the study with long strides.

The cats had found their way into the room. Samson snoozed before the fire. Delilah peeked from under the kneehole desk.

Agatha hadn't left the window bench. He crossed the room to her but didn't retake his seat beside her. He leaned against the bookcase and crossed his legs at the ankle.

"The man was worthless," he judged. "Less than worthless. If any evidence is found, we'll have to come up with it. Any confession will have to be forced out of O'Malley or your cousin."

She looked up at him. Her periwinkle eyes looked shadowed. Her mouth twisted. "And if my cousin had nothing to do with Stanton's death?"

"Why else would he have O'Malley torch the place, if not to reveal the body and cause problems for you? Do you think that constable will have the guts to go to Ipswich and look into your cousin?"

"I did not know Richard ever knew that I was involved with Stanton."

When she said the man's name, Jess felt a pang in his chest. For a decade she had thought the man abandoned her. To have that belief up-ended—what must she feel? "I guess finding him murdered changes the way you remember him."

"In some ways, yes. In others—. He'd known about the baby for a month. I told him as soon as I realized. I expected—I don't remember if I expected an immediate proposal. I do remember how shocked he looked. He told me he needed to marry money." She said the word as if it had a vile taste. "I had the farm. It grants a certain self-sufficiency. My mother left me funds on the 'Change that gives me independence. I realized after he was—gone," she swallowed, "that he must have meant he needed to marry lots of money. His brother confirmed it, that I do know. Aunt Sally told me. I don't think Stanton would have married me. I don't know the reason he lingered as long as he did."

"Waiting to talk to your cousin."

Her eyes re-focused, and he liked her back in the present, not in that shade-filled past. "You do believe my cousin murdered him."

"It lines up. He had O'Malley here, watching that no one else scarfed you up."

"And the vicar, telling me I should marry my cousin," she reminded.

"Did he now? I remember. At Christmas, wasn't it? You should have snapped his head off the way he'll barely shake hands after Sunday sermon."

She grinned, but she picked back up the thread. "Burn the cottage—kill you as his replacement, a neat bit of revenge, and reveal the old murder—but to what end?"

"You at sixes and seven, caught back up in the past, not looking at what's around you, waiting for your cousin to leave his warehouse and come courting."

"Then we should expect him soon?"

"Or not. Better to let things go off the boil and cool a little bit, then show up when nobody's thinking about you."

"Is that the way smugglers work? I don't think my cousin is that wily."

"Aye, he's that wily, trust me."

"Do you know him? I thought you said you'd met him a few times only."

Jess thought fast, harking back to the truth he'd limited himself to. "I said I know him, but we ain't mates."

"Yes, I remember now." But she still frowned.

He put a finger on that frown and smoothed it up. "Why did you ask if Lord Chalmesley had a reason to delay his constable's arrival?"

"Since Richard had O'Malley here and enlisted the aid of the vicar,

I guessed Richard would have contacted Chalmesley. Richard is the last male of the Helmes line. We never had a title, but it's an old family and once greatly respected at court."

"Elizabeth the First," he recalled.

"Yes. Lord Chalmesley would have that in mind when he was deciding what to do about my letter. I depended upon that to get us a constable, but I didn't predict—. He must have consulted Richard. His lordship might not know of my cousin's dealings with smugglers."

"I never said—."

"No, you didn't. I put a few bits together. Circumstantial, our constable would say, and not evidence."

Jess pursed his lips then allowed, "Still damning because it's the truth."

She looked up, her periwinkle eyes wide. "Well then. We know my cousin has criminal tendencies, even if Constable Evans and his lordship do not."

"Would your cousin have put a bee in his lordship's ear? That would prove that Helmes wanted the body found. So we ask why he wanted the murder uncovered. That seems to make him not guilty of it. Guilty of knowing about it afterwards, but not the doing of it."

"So much time has passed, can we ever know the truth about Stanton's murder? It's been ten years, Jess."

"You sound like that constable with his evidence and confession, not circumstance."

She bit her bottom lip. He watched her mouth. When she released her lip, it was reddened. It would be red like that when he kissed her. Not for the first time he wished that their New Year's kisses had been at the house. She'd been shivering with cold, but hot, so hot. Then Georgie had called out, and he had had to end the embrace or risk a kick to her reputation. Gossip already linked the two of them, especially since he and his ma hadn't made shift to move into another place. They remained in the house. And her past indiscretion kept coming up.

"Jess, what if it is not as convoluted as we have made it?"

It took him a moment to surface from his thoughts and puzzle out what her words were. "You mean that O'Malley burned the cottage to get back at me, and the body under the stair was nothing to do with either him or your cousin. Then we just need O'Malley for the arson."

"And the attempted murder of you and your mother." She shuddered. "You nearly died in there."

"We got out," he said gently. "No murders, just the arson. The murder was years ago. And the man who killed him—."

"Or the woman. Constable Evans is no doubt considering me."

"Not you," he said firmly. "If you had murdered him, then you would have known where the body was hidden. Guilt didn't make you swoon. That was shock."

"Shock that the body had been found."

"No. Don't think that way. The man or woman who killed him will be ten years' safe. How will they react when they hear the body's found, with a bullet in the skull?"

"I fainted."

"That wasn't a faint."

"I fainted from shock," she persisted.

"Not at finding out it was Stanton Myers or of getting his ring handed to you. Cold that was. You reacted to the finding of a body. You didn't know whose body it was. If you had murdered him, you would have known where that body was hidden."

"Unless I killed him and someone else hid the body and never let me know where."

Why did she continue to push that she had killed Stanton Myers? "Did you kill him?"

"No." Her eyes didn't flit away. "I thought about the ways I would do it if he ever came back. A bullet was not one of my choices. Slow poison. Something like poison mushrooms. Or a festering wound when I cut off his—well."

"Remind me never to make you mad at me."

She smiled faintly. "I didn't want to hurt him before he left." Her smile died. "Before he was murdered. I was still starry-eyed, more fool me."

"Not so starry-eyed. He could have planned to marry you."

"Then he was killed to stop his marrying me." She shook her head and massaged her temples. "It's an endless circle that makes my head hurt."

"It irks me to admit that constable's right, but he is. Without evidence, we've got nothing to work with."

Agatha rubbed her temples again.

"We need to drop this. Naught we can do but run circles around ourselves until we're spun tight in our own web."

Chapter 8 ~ Wednesday, 5 February

Agatha dreaded telling Aunt Sally of the constable's visit.

The woman was righteously angry that O'Malley would not be arrested for arson. "No evidence? No evidence! I guarantee he made a few wild comments to his mates in the pub. That constable should be questioning them, not you."

She bit her lip. "That's not the worst of the news, Aunt Sally. This is more disturbing, much more. The constable searched through the ashes. I don't know what he thought he would find, but he had a rather gruesome discovery. A body. All these years in that cottage. The body wore Stanton Myers' ring. He'd been shot in the head."

Aunt Sally merely raised her eyebrows.

Agatha stared at her. "You're not upset? Stanton didn't abandon me. Someone *murdered* him then stuffed him in the storage space beneath the stairs. He's been dead for ten years while I thought him off somewhere, gulling more young women. But—he wasn't. He was in that cottage—dead. And you're not upset."

"It's ten years past. I wanted him out of your life, Agatha. He was hurting you. He wasn't going to marry you. Yes, I knew you had told him. Weeks passed, and he still hadn't proposed—he needed to be gone. I was glad when he was gone. I thought he left, just as you did. I am a little dismayed that he was murdered. Are you upset, Agatha?"

That was a question she hadn't considered. Jess was right. She had swooned at hearing about the body, not that the body belonged to Stanton. "Less than I thought I would be," she admitted. "But do not be so—so satisfied around others. They might believe you had a hand in his murder."

"Not I. I didn't think of that as a solution."

"Do you know of anyone who thought his death was a solution?

"I know Robbie did not. He wanted him gone as well, so you would stop crying. Or him married to you. Although my brother thought your marriage would be as much of a mistake as Caroline marrying your father. Doomed to unhappiness, he said. We didn't want him dead, though. It has been—what? Ten years? I'm surprised the body could be identified, especially after that fire. How did the constable identify him?"

"Stanton's signet ring was still on—on his finger. The constable removed it and showed it to me."

"The ring. Yes, Stanton would never have given that up. His family's ring, wasn't it? A special heirloom. I had forgotten that." Samson jumped into Sally's lap. She stroked him, from head to tail, and soon his purring rumbled out. "You have had longer than I to consider everything. What are your thoughts?"

Agatha's mouth twisted. "Just that I have had plenty of thoughts. None of them will come to anything without evidence. As Constable Evans repeatedly said."

"And the burning of the cottage?"

"A similar circumstance. No arrest without evidence."

"That is the reason he left without making an arrest. I did wonder."

"We are left with two crimes, Aunt Sally, seemingly unrelated and years apart—and no one to be held responsible for either."

"Most unsettling." She continued stroking Samson. The purr continued through the room, soothing even Agatha's agitated nerves. "Well, Agatha, I only have one more question. What did Jess Carter think of the constable bringing up your memories of Stanton Myers?"

She picked at the loose thread on her skirt. "I didn't notice."

"Did you not?" Aunt Sally's dry tone emphasized her skepticism. "I suppose you could have been looking the other way. Have you noticed that neither he nor his mother have pushed to remove to another cottage?"

"There is no other cottage. As steward, he would have spotted that."

"The head gardener's cottage is empty. It's a little farther from the house, but still of a good size."

"Mrs. MacDonald and her grandfather live there."

"Or the Marshall's cottage, closer to the village. Wait, don't tell me, it's under lease to the Oxford don. Who only comes in the summer months." She beamed when Agatha scowled at her.

"It doesn't do to tease me, Aunt Sally. Neither of them has spoken to me about moving out of the house. Have they spoken to you?"

"Of course not. Mrs. Carter seems quite happy in her new domain, and the meals cannot be improved. She did ask for another helper since Mrs. Teller's girl is fit for nothing but the scullery. Tassie's oldest might be willing to be cook's help. I said I would ask you."

"It's up to Mrs. Carter. It's her kitchen now. I hope she will continue to join us at table."

Aunt Sally tilted her head. Her eyes had a strange gleam. "Mrs. Cabot never joined us."

"Mrs. Cabot was not a friend first, employee second."

"And Mrs. Cabot did not have a good-looking son."

"Aunt Sally! That is not driving any of my decisions."

"Do admit that he is good-looking."

"I freely admit it."

"Such nice broad shoulders. And he is so strong. He lifted that trunk I wanted brought down from the attic all by himself."

"Aunt Sally—."

"His hair and eyes are not remarkable, but that adds to his charm, doesn't it? And he has the best smile."

"Aunt Sally!" She stomped her foot for emphasis, and her aunt subsided with a smug smile.

"Has he expressed a wish to leave the house?"

"No, but I expect the request daily."

"Why? You said he would have noticed that no cottage is available."

"They were eager to get into their own cottage."

Aunt Sally shook her head. In a sage's voice she said, "I imagine the fire has them a little more reticent."

"Whoever burned the cottage could easily burn the house," Agatha pointed out.

"Don't say that! Don't put that idea into the world!"

"I never said a word," and she solemnly snatched the air and tossed it over her left shoulder.

They laughed. When the giggles subsided, her aunt nodded, as sagely as before. "Have you developed a *tendre* for our new steward, Agatha? Please tell me you have. You could do much worse."

Agatha shook her head. She refused to deny or admit it, God help her. She either had a broken heart in store or a marriage as socially unacceptable as her mother's second one to Robbie Wellesley. After a miserable first marriage to an earl's nephew, Caroline Fellows Helmes had been much happier in her second marriage to a simple farmer. Agatha wouldn't tempt fate by rushing her fences.

.~.~.~.

Monday, 17 February

Her cousin Richard had no difficulty with rushing his fences. Agatha scowled at his letter.

He'd obviously met Constable Evans, for he knew the name of her new steward. Or perhaps the vicar had finally dared to put the name on paper, having accepted that Reece O'Malley would not return to his former position.

*Don't think you can pull anything on me,* Richard wrote. *I have met this Jess Carter. He has my approval to work for you.*

He knew Jess, from the smuggling, she reminded herself. He probably thought he could use that knowledge against Jess. He wouldn't know that Jess had confessed his past to Agatha. *He's just waiting for a chance to turn Jess to his own purpose and away from me. He's my friend.* Then she mentally kicked herself. Her tall steward went out of his way to keep distance between them. Only yesterday he had reminded her that he was her employee.

That statement had depressed her—until he chucked her on the chin hours later when she stopped him to ask about the newborn calves.

She needed to ensure that Richard had no opportunity to contact Jess. Just because he had known Jess in his smuggling days did not mean that he knew him now.

He couldn't turn Jess into the authorities. Jess had said no writ was issued for his arrest. Richard couldn't very well testify that Jess had hauled freight for the smugglers without involving himself as receiving that smuggled freight.

And Jess had also said that he was no mate of Richard's. He had said that so clearly it seemed a given that he didn't like Richard.

She picked up the letter.

*I put a flea in that constable's ear. He interrupted me in my business and refused to come back after hours.*

Agatha grinned. Jess' information that Richard was a fence for smugglers had canted her view of her cousin. The constable had probably arrived when he was least wanted, probably because a nefarious deal was being planned. Nor had Evans toadied to her arrogant cousin Richard. She could almost see the steam coming out of her cousin's ears.

She skimmed the rest of the letter. Richard didn't ask about the burned cottage. He totally ignored the body found in the ashes.

She could barely remember his visit early in her romance with Stanton. She had heard him arguing with Robbie about it. She hadn't cared then, and she had thought he realized he couldn't control what she did. *But did he start planning how he could intervene? Had he planned murder?*

No evidence, Evans would say.

The letter ended with a few veiled threats that she would regret any hasty decisions. *I am here when you need to consult with me. I have funds to rebuild the steward's cottage should you wish to utilize them.*

Agatha nearly laughed aloud. She had needed funds two years ago, and Richard hadn't offered them. She had dug herself out of the pinch by tightening the reins and putting off the purchase of new stock. A surprising uptick of the `Change had helped. Now that she no longer needed money, Richard was willing to give it.

No, any money from Richard wouldn't be a gift. He would hold the money over her, expecting repayment, even if it wasn't in cash.

Her mouth twisted. She got up and threw the letter in the fire.

.~.~.~.

Wednesday, 4th March

The vicar settled in his chair. He sipped his tea. "I did receive a letter from your cousin."

"You probably should not tell me its contents, Rev. Rampling. The last time we discussed my cousin and his letters, you left in a bit of a hurry."

Aunt Sally snorted. Jess cleared his throat, and his mother merely handed her son another sandwich.

"Ah, well, your cousin is concerned for your welfare, Miss Helmes. He has only the best interests of the farm at heart."

"The best interests of the farm? That's rich." Aunt Sally then bit into her biscuit and had to chase the crumbs that fell.

"Did my cousin wish to know how the investigation into the burning of the cottage was going? No? Perhaps he asked about the investigation into the body found in the ashes? Not that either? Tsk, tsk." Agatha sipped her tea and eyed the vicar over the rim of her cup.

He shifted uncomfortably.

And Delilah dug her claws into his ankle.

"Yowch!" He sprang up. The tea sloshed out, his biscuit dropped to the floor, and Samson pounced on the sweetness. While Delilah calmly washed her paw.

Jess snorted.

Agatha re-filled the vicar's cup. He shifted to another chair.

"Do tell us what Richard Helmes had to say?"

"Aunt Sally, I did ask the Reverend not to tell us the contents of my cousin's letter."

"Ah, um, well—."

"I heard there were twins born in the village," Mrs. Carter offered as a potential conversation-starter.

The twins were talked of, their parents were talked of, their lineage was tracked. Other twins in the village were brought up. The church's new roof was mentioned. And Delilah crept under the vicar's new chair.

He stood up. "Um, ah, I do believe that I must get back. We have a church council meeting tomorrow."

"Yes, you must plan for that, I am sure." Agatha stood and offered her hand. Aunt Sally lifted Samson from the floor and stroked his back. The cat started his loud purring. Mrs. Carter gathered up the tea things.

Jess stood. "I'll see you out, vicar. Did you want to see the headway we're making on clearing the big beams from the burned cottage?"

"Can you re-use the beams?"

"Denny figures we can split the beams and use them for firewood or fence posts, one or the other." Still talking, Jess walked him out the front door.

"That went well," Mrs. Carter said.

"Good cat," Agatha said and snuggled Delilah beneath her chin.

. ~ . ~ . ~ .

Thursday, 19 March

The letter from Greville Myers arrived unexpectedly. Agatha stared at the seal, wondering who had written. When she broke it open and unfolded the letter, she looked immediately for the writer, then stood dumbfounded, staring at a name she hadn't seen written for years.

Stanton Myers' brother had first offended her with his cold rejection when she had written searching for news of her missing lover. His appearance after her baby's death had not registered with her. Robbie had dealt with him, and she hadn't cared.

He had written about a year later, telling her that he still had not heard from his brother. She had flung that letter into the fire.

She was half-a-mind to do the same to this one. She had rather enjoyed flinging letters into the fire in the past few weeks. Three of Richard's letters had burned quite quickly. After all, she had the Rev. Rampling if she needed to know what her cousin was thinking.

If her cousin could think outside his normal three statements. First, *Don't trust anyone I don't want you to trust.* Second, *I have the best interests of the farm in heart.* Third, *Don't fall for anyone when I plan to marry you years from now.*

With the sun warming her shoulders, she laughed.

But she turned to the first page of Greville Myers' letter and began reading.

He thanked her for the care she had taken to return his brother's remains. She had paid for a good casket as well as the hearse and accompanying outriders that carried Stanton from Helmesford to his home in Wellesbourne Montford, a journey of more than a week. Her explanatory letter had arrived a few days before the hearse, and he appreciated her explanation of events. The knowledge of what had happened to his brother was disturbing.

Then he addressed the arrival of Constable Evans. The man had returned the family signet ring to him. He conducted a long interview of Greville and his father. The sisters had long since married and moved on, but they would have had nothing to add to Greville's information for the constable.

*My own interview with Constable Evans was limited, although he asked the same questions in different ways several times. I could tell him little except that my father would not have sanctioned a marriage between Stanton and you. I shrink from writing these words to you, but they are no less than the truth.*

*When Stanton disappeared, and he obviously was not going to return, the recovery of the Myers fortunes fell to me.*

Agatha did remember a notice in the Times, announcing the betrothal of Greville Myers to some sort of American heiress. She wondered if he were satisfied in his marriage.

*You know that I visited a few months after Stanton's disappearance. I told your stepfather that my brother would not have left a young lady in such straits. I hope he conveyed that to you. That truth has now been revealed with the finding of his remains. While I join you in this fresh grief, I am gratified that my faith in my brother was well placed.*

*Stanton is now buried with his parents*—that was information Agatha would rather not have learned. *The mystery of his disappearance has resolved issues with the inheritance on my end. From Constable Evans I understand that the mystery of his murder is yet to be resolved. Evans has promised to keep me apprised of the progress of the case.*

If evidence is ever found, Agatha added wryly.

*We Myers hold fast, and so I shall until my brother's murderer is brought to justice.*

Was that a threat? Did he think she had done Stanton in?

*As ever, Greville Myers.*

The nerve of the man, thinking she was responsible for his brother's death.

Then she laughed.

"He's clutching at smoke." Much as she and Jess had done. The irony was that the constable's adage of *evidence or confession before arrest* now gave a certain relief. Greville Myers would have appreciated Evan's implacable stance on that as little as Agatha had.

Chapter 9 ~ Thursday, 26 March

Life returned to the slow tenor of days on the farm.

Rain then snow then rain washed away the soot and ashes at the steward's cottage. People gradually hauled away the charred timbers to cut up for their own fires. The cottage's bricks found their way into dozens of uses.

The fields were fertilized with manure turned deep into the soil to enrich it. Fences were mended; stone walls, rebuilt. Stored hay was carted out to the cattle. Early greens sprouted within the protection of the walled kitchen garden and under cold frames and withy baskets.

The house smelled of Mrs. Carter's baking. Aunt Sally and the maids turned out the napery and bed linens then stitched repairs in a sewing circle. The cats routed mice that crept in from the cold.

February worked through its deep winter and looked toward the greeny springing of March.

Agatha had followed her stepfather's habit of riding over the farms once a week to check the fields and livestock. While O'Malley was her steward, she had kept her ride solitary, but from the beginning Jess accompanied her. Gradually he convinced her to reduce the ride from a single all-day excursion to two half-days and then three half-days.

Riding behind her, Jess snatched off his stocking cap and jammed it into a pocket. He was having a hard time keeping his gaze off Agatha's long legs, encased in a man's britches for the first time. After last week's constant battle between the gusting wind and the long skirt of her habit, he'd suggested the britches would be easier. He hadn't really expected her to take that suggestion. Then, this morning at breakfast, she had diffidently asked for a regular saddle for Jenny, her usual mount. Even with that warning, he hadn't expected her to come skipping down the stairs in britches and her riding boots, showing a length of slender leg that messed with gut and brain.

His gaze had lingered on her long, long legs longer than it should have, then he had the added difficulty of the pretty shape of her bum when he followed her through the kitchen, out into the garden, and over to the stable.

Little Mike, holding the horses, was too young to appreciate the sight of tall Agatha Helmes in britches. Old Denny had whistled once then headed back into the stables.

Jess had thought she'd missed his uncontrollable reaction. He had cupped his hands to give her a boost up instead of leading her horse over to the mounting block. Her hand resting on the saddle, she suddenly stopped.

He glanced up. Her cheeks had flushed. He realized she had spotted his reaction, and it had flustered her.

"I can use the mounting block."

He wiggled his thumbs. "Here I am waiting."

She hesitated. Her gaze flickered over his face. When he didn't move, she put her boot in his linked palms. He tossed her up, getting a close-up view. She gathered the reins then guided Jenny in a circle around the enclosure while he mounted. "Look at that sunshine! It's glorious."

Jess eyed her seat in the saddle and worried for her. Agatha was a good horsewoman, but if she wasn't used to the saddle—. "Have you ridden astride before?"

"Not for a few years, but it's safer than the side saddle. Can we have a gallop when the horses warm up? We're going to the far field, aren't we? And it's such a glorious day."

He swung up on Big Clive. "The ground's still frozen. Your landing won't be soft."

"Oh, spoilsport. Surely you want a gallop as much as I do?"

"Big Clive is good at a canter. His gallop might shake my teeth loose."

She bared her teeth at him. "Jenny goes smooth as cream. So, is it a gallop?"

"It is."

"Yes!" She urged her filly along the alley between the stone outbuildings.

Beyond the buildings' shelter, the wind hit, reminding that it was still winter. An easy jog took them past other buildings, then a trot took them to the pasturage. Once through the gate, she set her heels to Jenny and let her fly. Big Clive came slower with his bone-rattling gait.

At the end of the far field, Agatha halted Jenny and turned back. Jess set Big Clive to the slope and had topped the knoll by the time Jenny reached the base.

Big Clive's bone-rattling gait had given him time to think. Through January and February he had strictly controlled his reactions to her. The reins had slipped this morning, and he had apparently shocked her.

Had she forgotten that New Year's kiss? Since then, she had treated him with calm efficiency that slotted him back into the box of her steward and nothing more. She might give him and his mother house-room. She might invite them to her table. But he had no doubt that Agatha would dismiss him if he even stepped close to the line.

Yet she tempted him more and more. Daily he fought the need to touch her. He stood close so she had to brush past him. He sat close when they pored over the ledgers. Her color would flame up, but she hadn't limited their contact. He longed to scoop her up and kiss her even more deeply than he had at New Year's.

His arousal had surprised her.

She hadn't seemed shocked, though. She was no virgin debutante, but a farm woman who'd had a lover and borne a child. Had his attraction surprised her? Or had his unabashed acceptance of it surprised her?

What else was he supposed to do except accept the temptation she was?

Jess had had trouble from the start. Him, hankering after a Long Meg who was ten times better than he was.

He couldn't even share his quandary with his ma.

He rode up to her. Her hair had slipped its ponytail and blew around. The sun lightened it to spun gilt. Her cheeks and nose and lips were reddened by the wind and cold. And her thighs gripped the horse tightly. He groaned.

"That was wonderful!"

"Was that the ride you needed?"

"Oh yes." She beamed then turned to look around the farm from this elevation. "It swept away the cobwebs."

"You looked like you've always ridden astride. I couldn't have kept up if I had tried."

She slapped Jenny's neck. "I used to ride astride with my stepfather. He kept a big hunter, and we would tear across the fields—."

She bit her lip, and Jess remembered that a riding accident had crippled her stepfather. "You can ride astride with me anytime." Only when the words were out did he hear the double meaning.

She didn't hear it. "For a while, but when it warms up, other people will be riding. I couldn't possibly—."

"It's your farm. Seems like you can do what you want on your own farm."

"It doesn't quite work that way, Jess. If I want to break propriety in one way, I can't expect to do so in other ways. I would be ostracized, and I don't want that."

"Are you planning to break propriety then, besides wearing britches and riding astride?"

She didn't answer. She just gave him her profile as she looked out over the fields.

He considered that balance. Today's ride gave him a glimpse of the young Agatha, before disgrace and death had damaged her. An eagerness for each day, a full-tilt rush into the world. She must have been a handful.

Since his arrival, she'd added a few pounds. Her eyes didn't look hollowed. He imagined the young Agatha would have had a silken layer and a bit more to hold onto. Just since he'd arrived, he'd seen her pick at her food when worries crowded her. Three deaths—her mother, Stanton Myers, and then her baby—those had shadowed her. They were followed by the last three years of her stepfather's life. For years stress would have reduced her to eating like a bird. He liked her long and slender. He could gather her up and—.

He had to stop. He couldn't think of her like that. She wasn't his, much as he wanted her to be. It was a dream. She might treat him as an equal and say she had no trouble with the past he'd confessed to her, but that would only last if he stayed in the steward's boots. She wouldn't want a smuggler for a husband. Her family had had this farm for hundreds of years. What would she want with a homeless wagoner? He certainly had no fine name like the man she'd expected to marry.

God help him. He needed to forget that New Year's kiss. What he had for Agatha was ten times, a hundred times worse than his imaginings about Katie Charteris.

"You've done well, Jess."

He ruffled his hair. "We've done well, Agatha."

She fiddled with the reins. "Without you I could not have accomplished any of this. I know; I tried. You have more fields prepared than we had last year. But—." She glanced at him. The wind blew hair across her face. She raked it away with her gloved fingers. "I don't want you to think I appreciate you only for the work you do on the farm. I've truly enjoyed having you and your mother at the house. Our conversations and—well, they've meant a great deal to me."

Her color stayed high throughout, but her gaze never wavered. He didn't know what to say. He settled for "I thank you, Miss Helmes."

"Miss Helmes? I thought we had dispensed with that long ago."

"Agatha. I look forward to our conversations, too. We rub shoulders real well with the work, too. There's a lot to farming a place this size, more than I ever knew. I only ever had charge of Ma's kitchen garden. I like learning from you."

She grimaced. "You make me sound like a grammar school spinster."

"My grammar school spinster had me wanting to kiss her." The words popped out, and too late he realized how they would reveal his attraction.

Those periwinkle eyes never faltered. "That is the best compliment I've had all year."

So, she wasn't going to haul him over the coals. "If you didn't stay so close in, you'd get more compliments like that. Better ones."

"From whom? The vicar? He would never dare. The squire is too old, his son too young. And his lordship is too married."

"That wouldn't stop some gentry nobs from chasing your skirts."

"Alas, I have no skirts today."

He dared again. "And I've appreciated it. You've got long legs, Agatha, and a man appreciates looking at them."

"Any man?"

*Is Agatha Helmes flirting with me?* "This man in particular."

That came too close to her hidden feelings. Her eyes averted. She gathered up the reins. But she had asked. And she had flirted a little.

*How out of practice is she? Have there been no beaux at all since Myers? Or before him?* He couldn't ask her. He certainly wouldn't ask her step-aunt.

"We should get back," she said and turned Jenny toward home.

"Another gallop?"

"Can you endure Big Clive's bone-rattling?"

"I'll do my best."

They didn't race. It was a canter, sometimes slowing to a walk as he pointed to work he thought needed done, and she explained a bit more of the farm's background or she waved to the few cottagers working around the estate.

He had to ask her about the workers that would be hired from the village, but he wanted Denny's view of the people before he approached her.

They rode past a wattle fence around an empty pasture, and Jess noticed the center was leaning. "Hold up, Agatha."

She drew up Jenny and took Big Clive's reins when he tossed them over. "What is it? Isn't this the field you wanted to put the new lambs and their dams in?"

"Aye. We spent a week building this fence." He reached the leaning post and gave it a shake before he realized it had separated from the ground. He bent to examine it.

"It should be sturdier than that. Who built it?"

"Denny."

"Denny builds better than that."

"He does. Someone sawed this post through, right at the ground. The one beside it, too." He straightened and squinted at the other sides of the enclosure.

"That's—that's sabotage."

"Aye, and dammit, it's work that'll have to be redone when other things are needed. I think there's three posts sawn through over there, and two over there." He pointed.

"None in the far fence?"

"Can't see. Maybe. Maybe not. I put Brutus the bull in the other field yesterday."

"Brutus does not take kindly to anyone."

"Wish we had more like him."

"You put him there yesterday? Do you think the posts were sawn through last night?"

"This fence was sturdy yesterday."

"And the posts didn't break?"

"Sawn through," he repeated grimly and came back to her.

Agatha's frown and primmed mouth told her anger, but she only said, "Denny will curse a blue streak." She handed over his reins.

"I want to myself."

"Don't let this woman stop you. It might alleviate my own anger."

He grinned, but the expression lacked his earlier ease. "This ain't the first bit of what I'd call 'sabotage', Agatha. It's just the clearest and the one that'll cost the most work."

"How long?" she asked when he'd mounted the Punch and clucked to him.

"What?"

"How long have you had to deal with this—. It's not a prankster, is it? This is more malicious. Vandal, I guess is the best word."

"Third time this month."

"And February is the shortest month. Is there a pattern? Every Thursday? Or every fifth day or so?"

"Not one I can reckon—or Denny either. His work's not been affected till now."

"You told Denny and not me." She sounded hurt.

"I told Denny 'cause I thought he might see something on his nightly perambulations. And I hoped it would stop. Village pranksters, needing to work off some spirits."

"It's not going to stop, though. Is it escalating?"

"Escalating? Does that mean getting worse?"

"Jess, how can you know perambulations but not escalating?"

"I'm a poor wagoner, Miss Grammar School teacher. Denny taught me perambulation. That's when he walks about."

"I know what it means, and yes, escalating does mean it's getting worse."

"Then that's the right word." He eyed the farm buildings near the house. The sun glinted on something metal in the opened doorway of the stable. Denny? But he'd thought the old man was heading into the village.

"Could our vandal have burned down the cottage?"

"You think O'Malley's back?" he asked.

"Who else would carry a grudge?"

"If he torched the cottage with me and Ma in it, I don't see him pulling pranks now. Sorry, Agatha."

They reached the stable enclosure. Jess called for Little Mike, but the boy didn't emerge. He slid off the Suffolk Punch and went to help Agatha, also sliding down. When her knees didn't catch, he caught her, his hands at her waist. The time for him to drop his hands and step back came and went.

She looked up. "Jess—."

Jenny bumped Agatha. She tumbled against him, landing against his chest. "Oof."

Jess set her back on her feet. "Do I have that much of an effect on you?" he teased.

"It was Jenny! She—oh, you!" Color high, she pushed off and took a step only to lurch to a stop.

"Agatha? What is it?"

"Hips that do not want to work. I'm not used to having my limbs spread out like that."

Did she realize the meaning those words could have? When she looked around, he saw her high color. Yes, she had, after the words were out. Much as had happened with him. Jess took pity on her. "You'll be sore tomorrow and even more so on Saturday. Maybe you should get in some more riding."

Her color flared higher, but she didn't back down. "I will." Then she hobbled away, the occasional 'ouch' drifting back to him.

Chapter 10 ~ Thursday, 26 March

"Well now. She's something to look at in those britches. And it's a come hither I ain't heard before but clear as can be."

The words came from the stable's shadows. In a voice Jess recognized. He had thought never to hear that voice again. Jem Webb. Captain Palmer's first mate, who killed for the smuggler then drank himself stupid to keep from remembering. Not arrested but walking free. Jess glared into the shadows. "You don't talk about her like that. She's a lady and my boss."

"Well, well, well. Ain't ye the cat's that's into the cream?"

He led the horses in and tossed Big Clive's reins at the man. "Make yourself useful, Jem."

The man grunted. "Which stall?"

Jess pointed it out and watched him lead the big Sutton Punch to the right stall.

Jem Webb. The last person he had expected.

He'd heard that Jem had been rounded up with the other smugglers at the Hawthorn Inn. Thrown into gaol, key tossed and waiting execution. But there was no mistaking Jem: his growl, his size, his stolid back, his grudging acceptance of a job.

When he'd finished with Jenny and came out of the stall, Jem was still working on the Punch, and Jess had still not figured out what he was going to do about the man.

Jem murmured to Big Clive, a steady undertone that had the horse near to dozing. Jess draped an arm over the wall then nearly guffawed when he heard Jem's words, a mixture of curses and sweet praises.

"I suppose you're wanting a job?" he asked when Jem headed out of the stall.

"I don't suppose ye've got a cushy one like yers?"

"Not so cushy. Up before dawn and all over the place during the day."

"And resting yer hands on that Long Meg."

"I warned you. I'm not afraid to plant you a facer, Webb."

"Ye'll be eying my knife if ye try." Jem dragged the blanket off the stall and eased it over Big Clive. The horse nuzzled his head. "Get off me," he complained, but the hand that shoved the horse back didn't push too hard.

"Where's the boy that's supposed to be here?"

"After I skerred him—."

"If you hurt him—."

"Nyah, no hurt. Just came up on him when he was kicking up his heels in a jig." Jem shook his head and grinned at the memory, although his twisted grin would scare anyone unfamiliar with his battered face. "He jumped a foot when I said I was looking fer ye. Told me ye were out with Miss Helmes. I told him I'd wait, since yer a mate of mine. That rounded his eyes. And I packed him off. He headed for the big house."

"Did you give your name?"

"Just Jem."

By that name alone his mother would know who had tracked them from the Naze. She had probably kept Little Mike in her kitchen, snaring him with cookies, to keep him safe from Webb. *Confirmed murderer*, he reminded himself, and Webb had turned to drink because of it.

In the dim stable light he couldn't see if Webb's eyes were clear or not.

"How did you find us?"

"I found Helmes in Ipswich. She's a Helmes. They related?"

"Some kind of cousin. When did you see Helmes?"

"Fortnight ago. He weren't friendly till I told him I was looking fer ye."

"The others were arrested in late October. Where you been?"

"Here and there, laying low." He struck a straw in his mouth and leaned against the stall door. He crossed his arms. At his ease, he didn't look like the authorities would have a warrant for his arrest. "Making plans."

And now came the reason Jem had tracked him down. "What plans?"

"I'm thinking the Colonies. Start new."

"The Colonies?" For a second the choice surprised him, then it made sense. A big land to get lost in, and not many people would know Webb's background. "Helmes Farm is a long way from a port."

"Ain't it, though?"

"What brings you here?"

"A couple of questions and a couple of needs."

Jess didn't like that sound of that. "What are they?" he snapped.

Before Jem answered, they heard someone running on the bricks of the stable enclosure. Jess swung around as Little Mike reached the open stable doors. The boy clung to the jamb.

"Your ma says the lunch is waiting. And to bring your friend."

Jem stepped up. "I ain't fit enough for the big house, boy."

"She said lunch in the kitchen and now." The boy ran off, probably to his own kitchen and already with a full belly, if Jess knew his mother.

"Your ma's still ordering you around."

"When it's her cooking, I don't argue."

Neither spoke as they walked to the house. Their talk would have to be private, and Jess didn't see that happening anytime soon. Not this afternoon, at least. Maybe tonight, after everyone was off to bed.

Which brought up where he was going to lodge the smuggler. He didn't dare ask Agatha to give Jem house-room. One, he didn't trust Jem. Two, he reckoned Agatha would put two and two to make four. She wouldn't want to give shelter under her roof to another smuggler.

Jem wouldn't appreciate sleeping in the stable loft while Jess had a feather mattress and a warm fire in the house.

"We need to talk."

"Yeh, that's sure. Private-like."

Then they reached the kitchen.

His mother poured steaming water into a metal pot sitting on the hearth slab. She straightened, holding the pot with a protective cloth. "Jem Webb," she said. "A face I didn't expect to see, far from home. Sit here." She tapped a chair at the scrubbed kitchen table. "You hungry?"

"As a horse. Nothing since last night. Mrs. Carter, ma'am."

Jess goggled at Jem on his best graces.

She put yeasty rolls before him. "Get started on that first. Jess, would you take those two pails up for Miss Helmes' bath? She's going to have a hot soak before her lunch."

He avoided the sly look he knew Jem would be giving him. Hefting the pails, he climbed up the back stairs and made his way to the bathing room. That was a luxury he had never encountered before Helmes House. He hoped that he never had to give it up.

He used his boot-toe to push open the door. Expecting to find it empty, he nearly sloshed the pails when he saw Agatha, dressed in a flannel robe. Her loose hair trailed over one breast as she stirred her hand in the hip-tub. The drawn curtains blocked the outside light, but lamplight cast a golden glow over the room and created a dangerous intimacy. A fire had barely warmed the room, and steam rose from the water. Another fire shot straight to his loins.

"I brought two more pails," he said inanely.

She unbent and turned to him, and Jess saw that the robe was all that covered her. He had a quick flash of her in the bath, her cheeks flushed from the steaming water, a long leg lifted to be washed. He needed to get out of here.

"Put them on the hearth to keep warm until I need them." Then her eyes widened, and he knew she'd seen his arousal. She pulled the robe's collar closer and held it at her neck. "Jess."

"I've got—I've got to get downstairs. You get—you soak. That'll take the soreness out."

He dropped the pails and headed for the door only to come up short when she said his name.

Then he realized that he couldn't leave with her not knowing about Jem's arrival. He had to warn her. He didn't dare look at her, not when he stood so close. He spoke to the half-open door. "I need to talk to you. Tell you—well, I've had a mate show up. He needs a job, a temporary one, before he's off to America."

"A mate? A friend of yours?"

He dodged the second question. "We worked together some."

"Smuggling?"

"That's it."

"Certainly you can give him a job."

He glanced at her and quickly away. "He's good with horses."

"Then there's no trouble." When he continued to hesitate, she asked, "There's more?"

"He needs a place to sleep."

"We have—."

"No," he said sharply and looked at her to be certain she understood. "He can't sleep here in the house."

Her eyes widened. "I thought you were vouching for him."

"No, I ain't vouching for him. He's dangerous, Agatha. I want him where I can watch him, but not in the house."

"You don't trust him."

"Not an inch."

She shivered.

Jess clenched his hands into fists and kept them at his sides. "We can talk later. After I've set him to a job, I'll come back and we can talk. He's downstairs now, eating. In the kitchen with Ma."

He took a step to leave but froze when she touched his arm. He stopped short. He was fighting to keep his hands off her, so he didn't dare turn to her. He could have that flannel robe stripped off in seconds.

"I've got to go," he growled.

She released him as if he was a dog that had snapped at her. He felt like a dog. "Thank you for bringing the water." Her voice was small.

He couldn't leave her thinking—he didn't know what she was thinking. He snatched her hand from the robe's collar. Damn, so close, and he with too much good sense. He rubbed his thumb over her smooth hand. "Agatha, you're too much temptation like this. I want—." He shook his head. It was harder to release her hand than he would ever have thought.

She smiled, and that didn't help. "I appreciate your honesty in all things, Jess. Your work, your past, and now."

"I'm not a good man, Agatha."

"You are with me. You are to me."

He growled. This time her feelings weren't hurt. Her gaze flickered over him, and her smile grew more like a cat into the cream.

Jess tore himself away and slammed the door behind him. He listened for her to lock the door, but didn't hear the click of the latch. Knowing he could go back and open the door and see her without that robe—he swore and tore down the stairs.

When he burst into the kitchen, his mother took one look and said nothing. Jem, his mouth full of thick stew, had no scruples. "She riled you up?"

"Shut up, Jem." He plopped onto a chair. His fisted hands pressed into his thighs.

"She ain't much to look at—."

"I said shut up. I'm warning you. I won't warn you again. She's a lady. You don't say nothing about her. You don't say nothing at all, not if you want my help. And you need my help, or you wouldn't be here."

"I'll shut it. This is good stew, Mrs. Carter."

She calmly set a plate and bowl before Jess. "How long do you plan to stay, Jem?"

"Wanting rid of me already?"

"We've made a place here. I don't wish you to disrupt that. And you will. I know you, Jem Webb. You won't take to a quiet steady life. Before long, you'll be standing drunk or fighting or both."

"You know me well, ma'am."

"Too well." She sat down and leaned her chin on her hand. "How long?"

"I need passage to the Colonies."

She glanced at Jess. "How much are you short? We have a little set by."

"No, Ma. We'll need that if we have to leave here."

Jem scowled. "And what would be causing ye to leave? Easy job and no quarrel with the lady."

"If someone lets our past become known, we'll have to leave. We already got a constable sniffing around. You saw the burned-out cottage. That was set, with me and Ma inside asleep. We nearly didn't get out."

"And they found a man's body in the ashes," his mother added. "So that constable will be back, what with an old murder and a new arson to solve."

Jem ignored the old murder. "They burned it with ye two inside? Ye ruffled somebody's feathers already, Jess?"

"We don't' know who set it."

"But you suspect someone."

Before he could stop her, his mother said, "A man named Reece O'Malley. He was fired as steward and the job handed to Jess on the same day."

"With help from the lady's cousin in Ipswich?"

"She don't know that. I told her I know him, but not that he'd sent me to her."

Jem leaned back and tore apart another roll. He popped a piece in his mouth then spoke around it. "Well now, if that don't pinch in on ye. If she finds out—."

Jess didn't want his former mate to have anything to hold over him, but he wouldn't lie. "She don't trust her cousin that much. She'd fire me, and we'll all be out on our arses."

Jem grinned then popped more bread into his mouth. "That's good to know. I wouldn't want to put a foot wrong and mess up yer cushy job. Or yers, Mrs. Carter, though with yer cooking, ye could get a job anywhere. Even in America."

She folded her arms across her bosom. "I'm not looking to emigrate."

"So ye wouldn't encourage Jess to come with me."

Her gaze didn't waver from Jem's. "That's my son's choice. He's got a good opportunity here—if you don't mess it up. But I'm not tying him to my apron strings. He can go where he likes."

"Where he likes is right here," Jem countered, "what with that Long Meg upstairs tempting him."

Jess scowled around his mouthful of stew.

"I didn't say nothing bad about her."

He jabbed his spoon at his mate. "You say nothing at all, and I'll be happier. You said you had a couple of questions and a couple of needs."

"I need a job to earn the rest of my passage plus enough to get me started over there. I thought I could keep my head down here until then."

"I can give you work. I'll set you up with a place to stay, free. Ma can see you get meals here in the kitchen. What're your two questions?"

"Would ye come with me to America? It's easier going somewhere new when ye got a mate to watch yer back."

"Or watch at the corner while you steal."

"There's that."

"That's no life I want. What else?"

Jem scowled. "We could make a mint in America."

"Have to work there just as hard here. Harder. And I want a place to root in. I like it here. What else?"

Jem picked up another roll then leaned back again. "I want to know how ye escaped arrest." In the heavy silence that dropped, he stared at Jess who kept shoveling his stew in. The man looked at Mrs. Carter then back to her son. "Ye go off with Palmer and Katie and that Farraday, and Palmer goes over the edge of the cliff."

"He fought Farraday on the cliff edge. Ground gave way under him."

"And what were ye doing?"

"What Palmer told me to. I kept a good hold on Miss Katie. I thought he'd win. Palmer always fought dirty. I was waiting on him to pull his knife. I didn't expect the ground to give way."

"Seems convenient: Palmer dead, everyone else arrested, and ye and yer mom gone."

"You weren't arrested. I heard you were. What happened with that? Who did you bribe to get out of gaol?"

"I was—elsewhere." His grin had a leer that spoke volumes. "They arrested old Jimmie, not me. A bit of luck that."

"We had the same luck and knew better than to test it. We were on the road before noon and never looked back." Jess paused. He put his spoon down and pushed his empty bowl to the side. "What did you tell Helmes in Ipswich?"

"Nothing. Said I was looking fer ye." And he grinned. "He said he had ye set up keeping watch on something fer him. That watch ye keeping on the lady?"

Jess refused to answer. His mother "hrumped" and gathered up his empty bowl.

Jem's grin widened. "He don't know ye want her fer yerself."

"She'll never have me. A smuggler? A common laborer? No."

"She knows ye were a smuggler? Ye told her? So she'll know I am."

"Exactly. She's already figured it out."

"Well, now, this is interesting. She's keeping that from the constable, ain't she? Looks like that wanting's going both ways. Nyah, I'm saying nothing else. Sit back down." But Jem's grin didn't fade. "This is a cushy job fer ye, ain't it?"

## Chapter 11 ~ Thursday, 26 March

Stiff muscles relaxed by the warm bath, Agatha reached for the linen sheet and climbed from the tub. She dressed slowly. Dreading her upcoming meeting with Jess' smuggler friend, she plodded downstairs and followed voices to the kitchen.

Mrs. Carter sprang up when she entered. "Miss, sit down here." She patted the back of her own chair. "We've got stew and bread, and I'll pour you some hot tea. These boys have nearly scarpered all of my rolls. I'll have to set more to rise tonight."

Agatha swallowed the tea first, nearly burning her mouth. The warmth from the bath had dissipated while she dressed. Wrapping her hands around the cup, she took her first good look at the newcomer.

A well-bashed face and a mouth made crooked by a scar, dark eyes impossible to read, and dark hair with touches of grey at the temples. Brawny and ham-fisted. She reckoned he'd been a fighter from birth. "You are Jem Webb, Mr. Carter's mate from his old home. We are glad of your visit, Mr. Webb."

"No visit. I plan to work here—."

"He needs to earn money for his passage to the Colonies," Jess intervened.

"To the Colonies? What an adventure! You are hardier stock than I, Mr. Webb. Have you decided on a job for him, Jess?"

Jess refused to look at her. He stared into his cup, swirled the remaining tea, then set it down. And still didn't look at her. "He works well with horses, Miss Helmes. Big Clive took to him right off."

"Then the stable it is. What of a place to stay?"

Jess started on options only to be interrupted by his smuggling mate. "When I was around the stables, I noticed the carriage house had rooms above. Looked like no one lived up there."

Agatha would have protested his prowling around, but she bit her tongue. The man had solved his own problem. "No one has stayed up there for years. We haven't had a coachman since my father's days. Those rooms are available."

"I'll just be needin' one of 'em."

"Whichever you select, Mr. Webb, it must be cleaned out and the chimney checked."

"It looked clean enough to me. A good sweep around will just do it. The chimney will be no trouble to open up and make sure it's clear."

"That's that then," and Jess drained his tea cup. Agatha thought the tension around his eyes had eased, and she guessed solving the problem of Jem Webb's living quarters had helped. She could not forget his grim expression when he'd warned her that his smuggling friend could not be trusted.

The men left to undertake the chimney cleaning. Agatha hoped Mrs. Carter would talk about Jem Webb, but the woman began gathering what she needed to make more bread.

She didn't manage to have a private word with Jess until his mother retired for the night and he announced that he would lock up the house.

From her upholstered chair beside the sitting room chimney, she looked up, unaware that the fire gilded her features. "We haven't locked up since that week after the cottage burned. Do you trust your friend so little?"

He took a couple of steps away. The movement gave her heart a pang. He'd kept a careful distance between them all evening. "He ain't a friend. I know him too well."

"Do you trust what he says? That he is here only temporarily, and that he'll be leaving for the Colonies?"

"I hope I can trust that. I hope he hasn't burned through his luck. He escaped arrest with the others by the veriest chance, but his name will be on the arrest warrants. He thinks they accepted someone else as him."

"But you do not think that? Sit down, Agatha waited until he sank into the chair cater-cornered to her. Still keeping his distance. He had not done so before Jem Webb's arrival. Or had she unnerved him when he'd brought the water for her bath? Those were not questions she could ask him. "So, Mr. Webb is sought for arrest. How did he find you?"

"The same way I found you."

"Ah, my cousin in Ipswich. Is Richard so well known to smugglers then? What does he do? Receive the goods they bring in and sell them on?"

"I didn't tell you that."

"But that makes the most sense." She tapped one finger to her lips. His gaze fastened on the gesture, so she repeated it. His hand fisted on the chair arm, then he looked away, into the fire. "My cousin must be making a tidy profit. I did wonder how his fortunes improved so drastically. I never would have expected him to—what do you call it? Receiving stolen and smuggled goods and selling them on?"

"He's a fence."

"A fence. Yes, that is how he is making money. I would not think there is a great demand for warehouses in Ipswich."

"His profits will have fallen off since October."

"That's when your mates were arrested? You and your mother fled, and Jem Webb did as well. Do you think any of your other mates escaped? Your leader?"

"He's dead. I saw him die."

He shifted in his chair. He'd grown more uncomfortable as she pursued her cousin's criminal enterprises. But he didn't refuse to answer her questions. Jess must want her to know the truth, as he had before she employed him. How much truth would he tell her? "So, Jem Webb cannot remain in England and plans to go to the Colonies. Which one?"

"Canada's my guess. He's not much for the hot weather of India or Africa. And he'll avoid Australia."

"Will my best steward go with him?"

He stilled and gave her a sharp look. "I never thought of doing that, Agatha. Unless you're disappointed in my work."

"Far from it, Jess." And now she had nothing more to say. She pressed her last point. "When will he go?"

"The best time for crossing is April and May. The longer he stays, the closer the law will come to finding him. We've already got a constable poking around. He'll stay about six weeks, I reckon. Now, I got a lot to get through tomorrow, things I put off this afternoon so I could deal with Jem. Good night."

She murmured "Good night" and watched him leave. In the bathing room she had watched him wrestle with his lust. He'd looked as if he wanted to grab her and kiss her silly. She had wanted it, too. Then he'd controlled himself and walked out, the very way he walked out now.

She should be grateful that he hadn't grabbed her up. She should be grateful that he was taking extra precautions with his nefarious smuggling partner on the estate.

She wasn't grateful. She flounced to her room like a spoiled child, where she tossed and turned for several hours.

.~.~.~.

Wednesday, 1 April

Nor was she grateful on the next Wednesday when the vicar invited himself for tea, proclaiming he was lured in by the chance of Mrs. Carter's currant scones.

His first words revealed his mission. "I hear your steward has hired a new man."

Agatha was proud that she displayed no uneasiness. She finished adding the three spoons of sugar that he preferred, poured the tea in, and handed it without a single rattle of cup on saucer. "Where did you hear that, Rev. Rampling?"

Her direct question flustered him. His tea cup rattled, and he had to set it down on the table. "I met the man myself at the pub last Friday night. Called himself Jem Webb."

"That is his name."

"He said he was an old friend of your steward Jess Carter."

"That is how Mr. Carter introduced Mr. Webb to me, as an old acquaintance. You did not think my new steward sprang out of the ground, fully grown and with no history? Or that Mr. Webb did so?" She leaned back and sipped her tea. "Mr. Webb is working in our stable before he moves on."

"His position is temporary then?"

She stirred her tea again and sipped it. Then she leaned forward to offer the plate of savory pasties that Mrs. Carter had made. The vicar took two then looked expectantly at the buttery scones. Agatha dutifully lifted that plate to him.

The actions gave her time to determine how much to tell the vicar. No doubt he would report their conversation to her cousin. He would not know that her cousin had directed Jem Webb to Helmes Farm, just as he had given directions to Jess Carter. She had never questioned the reason Richard sent two former smugglers to her property.

Perhaps she should contemplate that question a little longer.

She merely smiled at Rev. Rampling. "As Mr. Webb says. I do know that Mr. Carter is pleased with his work. He says the man enjoys working with horses. He says that perhaps his old mate has found his calling."

"He did not work with horses before?"

"I believe he did something with boats." Agatha tried to sound vague and uninvolved, as if Jem Webb meant nothing to her.

"I see. That means he was on the coast."

"I thought myself that he had been working on the rivers, perhaps hauling freight via the canals." She needed to distract him. "Have you corresponded recently with my cousin Richard? He sent a letter to me after Christmas. He and I are not great letter-writers, but I believe you have written him numerous times in the last few months."

"Me? Not I."

Agatha set down her teacup. "Come, Rev. Rampling. Do not shade the truth. You have received three letters from him in match to my single one. You have shared those letters with me. When you arrived today, did you not remind me that my cousin had recently sold several casks of wine to Lord Chalmesley? Did you not remind me a fortnight ago, as I left church, that my cousin would be a suitable match? I remember that conversation even if you do not."

"Um, ah, well—."

"I suppose that is his letter poking from your pocket?"

He clapped his hand to his pocket. When he felt no exposed letter, he gave her a frown. "You tease me, Miss Helmes?"

"With the truth, though, for you would not have believed me if you were not in the habit of stuffing letters in your pocket. Has my cousin recently written to you?"

"Um, ah, well."

"Come, let us have the truth. I will not snap your head off if you do not matchmake. Tell me of my cousin's inquiries."

"I—well, he was concerned with the body found in the burned-out cottage. Um, someone had informed me that the body was identified as a Mr. Stanton Myers."

Agatha set down her cup and poured more tea. She lifted the pot to him and poured when he eagerly held out his cup. "Have you become aware of Mr. Myers' identity, Reverend?"

"No one has told me anything about the man."

"Not even my cousin? Since you are a relative newcomer—hasn't it been only four years since Lord Chalmesley gave you the living here?—the information is old news to most in Helmesford. Mr. Myers was my beau. I expected to marry him."

"He was the fath—um, well."

"Quite so. I am surprised the gossips did not inform you. What did my cousin ask?"

"Um, ah, he wanted to know the circumstances of the man's death."

"Did gossip not carry that information to you?"

"Just that he was murdered."

"Shot in the head, according to Constable Evans."

"You must have been—you are not—you seem—."

"Any emotion that I would have felt for Mr. Myers faded long ago, Reverend. It is ten years since he disappeared, and we all thought he left to escape his responsibilities. I am quite sangfroid now."

"I understood that you fainted."

"The gossips did not completely fail you, then."

"No, well, um." He hid in his teacup.

Agatha stared into her tea. The amber liquid shimmered in the cup. "I was shocked that a body had been found. I fainted then. Perhaps I was fortunate to be sitting down when the constable handed a ring belonging to Mr. Myers to me for identification."

"You did not—um, the body—."

"Only bones."

"You are ... cold, Miss Helmes. A man is dead."

"Yes." She set aside her tea. "Stanton Myers is ten years lost to me. As I said, any emotion that I had for him faded when I thought he abandoned me."

"To discover his murder—."

"That was a shock, yes. Just as it is a strange relief. I wonder now if he might have kept his word, had a bullet not intervened."

"His word?"

"We did speak of marriage. Or did you think me a silly woman who falls for any man?"

Rampling hid in his teacup again.

"Tsk, tsk, Reverend. I am ten years older now. The gossips have not linked my name with any other man." When his expression changed, she more clearly understood the reason for his self-issued invitation to tea. "I see the gossips are linking my name with someone. Who do they think holds my heart now?"

"Um, ah, you have been seen, more than once, out riding with him."

"Mr. Carter? My steward?" Displeasure hardened her voice.

He almost cringed in his chair. "You are seen riding with him," he defended.

"We ride over the farm to check the work being done to prepare for planting. Surely, Rev. Rampling, you understand the importance of the spring plowing and planting? You are surrounded by farmers."

"You did not ride out with Mr. O'Malley."

"I did not trust Mr. O'Malley with my person. I was correct, was I not, since he assaulted me? Mr. Carter offers me nothing but respect."

"You did not ride out with Mr. Garner or Mr. Hurst."

"Mr. Hurst had no head in the morning. His soused head was the reason I dismissed that drunken swine. Mr. Garner did not often bestir himself to ride beyond the near fields. His sin was sloth. I cannot believe—yes, I can believe it." Agatha fumed for seconds. She started to explain Jess' lack of farming knowledge, but that would undermine his authority. "I trust you will scotch these rumors." His very stillness alerted her. "What else?" she snapped.

"You allow him to stay here in the house."

"The steward's cottage burned down. Mr. Carter and his mother nearly died in that fire. No thanks to Mr. O'Malley. Where else would the Carters stay? No other cottage on this whole farm is worthy of the steward."

"He stayed in this house before he moved to the steward's cottage."

"With his mother and my aunt as chaperon. As they continue to be."

"I believe she is your step-aunt."

"That's still two women to guard my reputation. I am shocked at you, Rev. Rampling. I act as a Christian and give house-room to two people, people that my cousin," she underlined the relationship, "sent to me for employment. Just as my cousin sent Mr. Webb to the farm."

"Mr. Carter and Mr. Webb are known to your cousin?"

"Indeed. Do write to him and confirm that information. You will discover I do not lie."

"Um, well, I never suggested you spoke falsely."

She tilted her. "Yet you never quite believe me. You always need confirmation. That disappoints me. I wonder: who else are you so misjudging?"

He straightened. She had finally managed to offend him. "Are you judging me, Miss Helmes?"

"Certainly not. A suggestion only." She stood. "I believe we have fully discussed your concerns now."

"Your cousin—."

She sat. There would be no budging the man until he'd finished his appointed duty.

"Your cousin expressed his wish that you would consult with him prior to finalizing any decision about the farm."

"My cousin is a merchant in Ipswich. He has never lived on a farm in his life. Only a fool would ask a merchant how to manage a farm."

"Mr. Helmes merely wishes to ensure the farm is kept secure. With your stepfather's death last year, you have lost the steady guidance of a man. Witness the three stewards you have hired and fired in one year."

"My cousin would have agreed that keeping Mr. Hurst and Mr. Garner employed would have been folly. Surely you support that position."

"I do, indeed, but—."

She rode across his objection. "All three stewards came with my cousin's recommendation." She slanted the truth here, just a little shave off the facts. Richard had placed the advertisement, and because he insisted, Agatha let him proceed. He had weeded through the applicants, leaving only one man each time to be interviewed. She, poor fool, had not divined his intent to undermine her and the farm until O'Malley's arrival. Bad luck. A bad read of the applicant. That's what she thought—until Reece O'Malley was so clearly unsuited. He knew the work, but he only pushed for its completion because she pushed him.

"Yes," the vicar nodded, "he does write that. But Mr. O'Malley was an excellent choice for steward."

"Mr. O'Malley made advances on my person. Mr. Carter intervened. My cousin surely does not want my personal safety to be in peril."

"No, of course not. But the farm——."

Agatha huffed, growing tired of his inability to grant her knowledge of her own land. "I am not likely to run the farm to seed, Vicar. You might assure my cousin of that. He apparently expresses his concerns to you and not to me. Please remind him that I have had the running of the farm in my hands since my mother's death a decade ago. My stepfather did give his advice, but the decisions were mine. As they should be." She stood again. "As the farm is mine alone. Not my cousin's."

"He states the farm is——."

"By my father's will and my grandfather's, and his father's and grandfather's, the farm lawfully descends to me. I inherited, Reverend. The property does not pass through the male line but through the firstborn legitimate heir. It is bequeathed, through the early days of the reign of Elizabeth I. You may view the documents, if you wish. Or you may speak with his lordship. I do apologize, but I may not devote more of my afternoon to you. I have pressing matters with the farm to decide. Do let me know when next you wish to come to tea." She tugged the bell rope.

Civility got him on his feet.

Jess emerged from the kitchen area. "Please have the vicar's trap brought round." Then she stepped into her study and firmly shut the door.

And leaned against the solid wood while she trembled with anger.

*How dare he! How dare Richard!*

Then she laughed. Typical of her cousin.

What would the respectable vicar do when he discovered his respected merchant of Ipswich was a fence for smugglers?

.~.~.~.

Jess opened the study door.

Agatha looked up from her ledger and scratch tally sheet. Her first frown smoothed away, but she did not greet him with her usual smile.

"Calmed down?" he asked.

She winced. "Was my anger that obvious?"

"He nattered on about your cousin and his questions about the farm. He kept apologizing. He was still apologizing when he climbed onto his trap."

She threw down her quill. "He believes everything my cousin tells him! He thinks my cousin has a say in the farm. He thinks I am an ignorant female who does not know how to run a farm. He thinks I exhibited remarkable idiocy in hiring and then firing a drunkard, a slugabed, and a lecher, in that order. He does not care that my cousin sent each one of them to me. He thinks that I must be involved with you, because I hired you and gave you and your mother rooms in this house, and because you and I go riding together."

By the time she finished she was pacing before the hearth.

"We'll move out tonight."

Agatha whirled around. "You will not!" Her finger stabbed the air. "You have nowhere to go, for one thing. I will not have the farm steward housed in a tiny cottage smaller than the workers that he gives orders to. Or a cottage needing new thatch and a rebuilt chimney. You will stay here, you and your mother. I am not embarrassed by his words. I am angry!"

"He said there was gossip in the village."

She flicked her hand. "This to that gossip. There is always gossip."

"If it did not matter to you, you would not be angry."

"The gossip does not make me angry. His claim that I cannot run the farm makes me angry. I would be able to run the farm if those imbecilic workers would listen to me instead—. I am infuriated that he believes my cousin has any type of ownership in the farm. He does not! My cousin is a fool if he thinks he will have one thimbleful of this land!"

"Agatha—Miss Helmes—."

She stamped her foot, and Jess wisely looked to see if she had anything close that she might throw. "Don't you dare call me Miss Helmes. I thought we were friends. Don't you dare change because my cousin has the vicar in his back pocket."

"Don't forget O'Malley. He's part of this."

"Of course, he was. Richard sent him. But he's gone now."

"He's still around."

"He is still here, in the village? Who has given him house-room?" She planted her hands on her narrow hips. "I'll fire them." With that gleam in her eyes, he thought she would.

"They're not on the farm."

She narrowed her eyes. "What do you know?"

"I know you can't fight a battle against rumors without making them more believable."

"I don't want to hear good sense, Jess. I want O'Malley gone from here!"

If he were an evil man, he'd get rid of the man himself. He wanted him gone as well. Within the bounds of the law, however, he couldn't do much. Not since constable was already suspicious. "O'Malley's off the farm. That's as far as you can control."

She heaved a sigh. Her hands dropped from her hips. She crossed her arms and hugged herself, as if she were chilled, even standing before the hearth fire as she was. "How do I get that vicar to listen to me and not my cousin? Tell me that. Should I go to his lordship?"

He shrugged. "If you involve Chalmesley, you merely prove that you are a weak and arrogant female."

Her mouth quirked, and Jess breathed a sigh of relief that her steaming anger was dissipating. "You could teach me how to bloody his nose."

"Oh, you'll shine then, a woman giving her vicar two black eyes."

Agatha stamped her foot, but she was smiling. "Stop being so reasonable, Jess."

"If you want to learn to hurt someone, Agatha, then I'll teach you. It might come in handy with your next steward."

Her smile vanished. Her fists clenched. "My next steward? Are you leaving me—the farm? Are you going to Canada with Jem Webb?"

"Wait a minute. I've got no plans to go anywhere with anyone. But who knows what the future holds?"

"You're doing well here. Your mother likes it here." She gulped. "I thought we discussed that. Mr. Camden my trustee even approves of you and the changes in the farm."

"We did discuss it. I told you then. I've got no plans to leave. I'm staying here."

"I don't want you—or your mother to leave. You're becoming like—like family."

"So, I'm your younger brother."

She blushed. "No. Far from that."

He hoped she'd say something else, but she steered around it, much as he did.

"You will teach me to plant a facer?"

"We can start tomorrow." Teaching her to hit might give him the opportunity to bridge the distance that kept coming between them.

"It is almost worth that hour with the vicar to learn how to bloody his nose." She sounded like she anticipated satisfaction. Jess wished he'd been a party to that encounter with the vicar. He might have hauled off and hit the man himself.

"Or to bloody O'Malley's nose."

She went very still. Her eyes narrowed. "You say he's in the district. Where, Jess?"

"No, you don't. You'll hare off after him, and he'll slip away."

"You're keeping a watch on him?" The question revealed her worry that O'Malley would strike again.

"Much as I can. He's elusive if he knows he's watched."

She nodded, accepting it. "Are we still having things go wrong? Like with that fence Denny built?"

"Not for the past fortnight."

"He's trouble."

"Don't I know it," Jess agreed. "But we've got no evidence. Thanks to that constable for telling us it will take either evidence or a confession to get someone arrested."

"You would have to bring up Constable Evans."

"Would you like to bloody his nose?"

She grinned, a full-on grin, not just a wide smile. "If the occasion permits," her prim tone at odds with that smile.

He laughed aloud.

"I would prefer to plant my cousin a facer."

"He's off in Ipswich. No opportunity."

"There will be opportunity soon enough."

"What's this? Is he coming here?" Would he expose Jess' main and only lie?

"He will, once the vicar delivers news of my unwillingness to bend to his will. You must remain my man, Jess. Not my cousin's."

"I'm not your cousin's man."

"I have your word on that? When he comes in, blustering and throwing slanders, you will remain not just the Helmes Farm steward but also my friend?"

He wished to be more than her friend. He wished he could tell her that. He considered her anger from the vicar's comments. She would be ten times worse than that with her cousin. And he would be revealed as Helmes' plant, not just an acquaintance, as he'd let her think.

"As you wish, Miss Helmes."

"Don't Miss Helmes me, Jess. I remain Agatha to you."

"It's too familiar. To go along with it, Ma and me are living in the house with you."

She huffed. "You sound like the vicar. You two are here, yes, along with my aunt Sally and her two cats. This house is not a den of iniquity."

"For those two cats it is. They sleep and eat. One of them was caterwauling with the barn tom. We'll have kittens soon enough."

She laughed. She needed to laugh more often. She should wear her hair down, the way he'd seen it in the bathing room. He hadn't gone to sleep that night until he'd taken himself in hand. The memory kept interfering with his farm work.

The memory alone woke his need. Seeing her, framed by the fire behind her, her head tilted to one side, her hair gleaming like a halo, her hands framing her small waist: he wanted to put his hands on her waist and pull her close and bury his face in her loosened hair, and know that they were more than friends.

Sometimes, he thought she wanted that as well. But he couldn't push himself on her. Or he and Ma would be back in their freight wagon, looking for another place to call home.

"So," she said, "you will teach me to fight?"

"Tomorrow," he promised.

## Chapter 12 ~ Friday, 3 April

Jess hexed them somehow, for Constable Evans appeared on Friday and wanted to speak with Jess. Agatha had yet to have her first lesson in boxing.

She had gaped at the man. Her fist formed, but she reminded herself that wanting to hit a threat to her world was not the same as actually doing it.

The constable had come at noon, just when they were to have soup and bread and cheese. Her stomach rumbling, she led him to the sitting room, then hied off to the kitchen.

"Where's Jess?" she asked as soon as she was in the warm room. Aunt Sally looked up from slicing bread.

Mrs. Carter turned from getting down plates and bowls. "At the stable talking to Jem. I heard someone come in. What's to do?"

"That constable has returned. He wants to question Jess."

Mrs. Carter paled, but she managed, "What would he want with my boy?"

Agatha didn't stop to answer but snatched up a cloak from the hook. She flung it around her as she sped between the rows of kitchen herbs and cloched lettuces.

Jem Webb was holding forth on the merits of cider over ale when she came upon them. He fell silent and merely stared. Discomfited as always, she focused on Jess.

"You cursed us."

He stood up from his hay bale. "How's that?"

"You brought up Constable Evans, and now he's in the sitting room. He's here to talk with you. He would not tell me more."

"Man sounds like a right nuisance," Jem said. "What's the best place to stash him?"

"Stash him?" Agatha gaped at Jem Webb then turned to Jess for explanation.

"Shut it, Jem. I'm not killing a constable."

He folded his arms across his broad chest. "I'm not headin' to gaol."

"Agatha, did anyone come with Evans?"

"No. He's alone."

"Best time to kill 'em."

"No. That's proof he's not here to arrest anyone. Stay here and keep out of the way of being noticed, mate. I'll deal with him."

Jem Webb scowled but remained on his hay bale. He grunted agreement. She wondered what the man would do if the constable came to the stables.

Jess caught Agatha's arm when she would have hastened back. "We're in no hurry. He didn't give you any idea what he wanted?"

"Just that he wanted to question you."

"We know he's talked to Greville Myers. We know he's been to Ipswich and talked with your cousin."

"Could he be the reason my cousin wrote to the vicar? My cousin wants to know where you are and where Jem Webb is. Could he have betrayed you two as smugglers?"

"Like I said, the constable came here alone. That means he ain't here to arrest anyone. Your cousin can't talk about smuggling. He'd have to explain how he knows what he knows, and that buys trouble for himself." He ushered her inside, drew off her cloak and hung it on the hook. "Go on in and talk to him."

"He wants—."

"I know. But we're not going to bite the first lure he throws out. Go on."

Agatha passed Mrs. Carter who had taken in some tea. "That man," she grumbled. "He had the gumption to ask for bread and a slice of meat. He's here to harass my boy. He'll get nothing more from me."

"Mrs. Carter—."

"No, Miss. I'll not be feeding him." She slammed the kitchen door behind her.

Agatha entered the sitting room to find the constable staring into his cup as if a foreign substance was swirling in the tea. He looked at her then slowly put the cup on its saucer. She offered a weak smile and sat down across from him, spreading her skirts over the settee.

"Did you warn him?"

She opened her eyes wide. "Warn him? I informed him that you were here and wished to speak with him."

"I hoped for a private word with him, Miss Helmes."

She straightened her spine, arched her eyebrows, and looked down her nose. "Mr. Carter is in my employ. I have a right to hear this interview, as you have an obligation to inform me of the reason for it."

"Nothing to disturb you, Miss Helmes."

"I am waiting, Constable Evans."

His mouth tightened. Then he gave a curt nod. "In the course of my investigation, it has been brought to my attention that your new steward

Jess Carter may have been involved in criminal activity."

She wanted to slump against the settee. Instead, she looked frostier. "Criminal activity? Where? When? Since he has entered my employ?"

"I have no evidence of that. The event would have occurred before he entered your employ."

"You do have evidence of a crime?"

"There was mention of smuggling."

"Mention of smuggling? From where did you receive this information?"

He reached for his tea, lifted the cup, remembered it with a shudder, and returned the cup to the saucer. Behind her, the door opened and shut. A long stride brought Jess into view. He took a station on the edge of the round carpet.

"May I guess my cousin is your source of information, Constable?" Agatha remained on defense. "Is my cousin accusing Mr. Carter because we accused my cousin?"

"Now, Miss Helmes—."

"Did he give you any evidence? Sit, Mr. Carter, and hear the latest from my cousin. He has accused you of smuggling."

"Smuggling, Miss Helmes?" Jess perched on a side chair. "I think not. Has your cousin accused me? I never thought that would happen, especially when he himself sent me here to seek employment. He's countered that good turn with a wrong one."

"How can he accuse you?" She glanced at Evans. "How can my cousin give any evidence of a crime without implicating himself?"

The constable leaned forward. His eyes gleamed. "Are you saying your cousin is involved in smuggling, Miss Helmes?"

"How would I know that, Constable? Would I not then implicate myself? How can I be involved in smuggling when I never leave my farm? That isn't possible."

Jess folded his arms over his broad chest and glared at the man. "Miss Helmes is not involved in anything criminal. How dare you suggest otherwise?" He started out of his chair.

Agatha stayed him with an uplifted hand. "My cousin accuses without foundation in retaliation for our accusation. Is that it, sir? As you told us before, you cannot arrest without evidence or a confession or both. I do not think you have received either. Good day to you." She stood, with Jess seconds behind her.

Yett Evans was of stronger mettle than Agatha had realized. He maintained his seat. He met her gaze steadily. A little smile played in the corners of his mouth. "A moment more, Miss Helmes, Mr. Carter. I am not totally without information, and Mr. Helmes of Ipswich is not my only source."

Agatha subsided. Jess remained standing, arms still folded, feet braced wide. "We are listening," she said.

Evans eyed the teacup like a thirsting man, but he didn't reach for it. Instead, he withdrew a folded paper from his pocket. The crackling as the paper unfolded sounded loud. He perused the paper then said, "A coastwatcher tells me that a man named Jess Carter worked with smugglers. He crewed with them. He hauled the smuggled goods inland for them. He intimidated witnesses for them. He worked with the leader named Palmer. His mate on the crew was Jem Webb, a known henchman who did Palmer's dirty work."

Jess looked down from his great height. "I did crew for Captain Palmer when Jimmie couldn't, but I never smuggled no goods into England, Constable." He kept his gaze steady. His color remained good. He lied well—which had Agatha wondering if she'd believed other lies without questioning them.

"We fished," Jess was saying. "Caught them legal, sold them at market. Palmer had other business, I know, but he never involved me."

"The man Palmer cannot confirm your statement. He died last autumn."

Jess blinked. Then he said, "The old man Jimmie was arrested with the rest of the smugglers."

"Yes." Evans' gaze remained as steady as Jess'. "I spoke with him. He seemed too old to crew any ship."

"What did he tell you?"

His mouth twisted. "Words that I'll not repeat before a lady. At the core, he said he'd turned up where he belonged to be."

"There is a 'but'," Agatha interjected. "I heard it. Tell us, sir."

"The court has experienced a bit of confusion about this man Jimmie, who is charged with smuggling. We hear of a man named Jem Webb. Jimmie claims to be Jem Webb. No one will say 'yea' or 'nay'. Some of us do not believe Jimmie is Jem Webb. His age is problematic. He sounds an old sea dog. He knows fishing, that is certain. But we do not believe he worked with the smugglers. We have more than a few threads to support our belief."

"You say belief, not evidence. Did you not tell us yourself that you will not arrest without evidence or confession, Constable? Also, you have not told us how any of this involves Mr. Carter."

"Bear with me, Miss Helmes. We have no active case against Mr. Carter, but those few threads tell us to keep looking for Jem Webb. The old man named Jimmie cannot be Jem Webb. Webb is not sitting in a London gaol. He is not on the Naze. Your cousin, Miss Helmes, claims that a man named Jem Webb came to him, trying to track you, Mr. Carter. He directed him to here. Do you know a Jem Webb, Mr.

Carter?"

"I do," he said, brazening it out. "He's no more of a smuggler than I am. We did crew for Palmer, fishing is all. I don't know of him doing any dirty work for the captain."

"Is he here, Mr. Carter? Is Jem Webb on Helmes Farm?"

"He was before I came to the house, aye, sir. We gave him a job. He's a mate. We grew up together. He's no henchman, though he might look it."

"That is for the law to decide, Mr. Carter."

"Is there a warrant for him? Is there one for me?"

Evans sighed and leaned back. "No warrant, not for either of you. I checked. Colonel Farraday and his wife spoke up for you, and who am I to doubt word of gentry folk?"

"Yet here you are," Agatha said, "still cautious, still asking your questions, hunting your evidence. Ignoring the arson of the steward's cottage, the attempted murders of Mr. Carter and his mother, the murder ten years ago of Stanton Myers."

"I am here, Miss Helmes. Here I'll stay until I have answers for all of it." He took another look at his teacup then folded his paper, tucked it away with the pencil and stood. "I've got room and board at the pub. I've got people who are keeping their ears to the ground for me. I can wait. Good day, Miss Helmes, Mr. Carter. I can see myself out."

Jess trailed him to the hall and shut the door behind the man. When he returned to the sitting room, Agatha was at the window, watching as Evans mounted his horse then turned the gelding for the ride back to the village.

Over her shoulder she said, "Jess, what are we going to do?"

"What we're doing. Come on into the kitchen. We need to eat."

She followed him. When they entered the kitchen, Jess' mother looked up from stirring the soup. "Is he gone then?"

"Good riddance," Aunt Sally said.

"He's just doing his job," Jess offered.

His mother shook her head. "You didn't do nothing wrong, Jess, not that wrong, and besides, Kate and Col. Farraday saw to it that nothing landed your way. They should leave you alone."

"I am guilty of some things, Ma, and you know it."

"Not like Jem Webb, and you know that."

"That new worker?" Aunt Sally asked. Under the table, Samson mewled. "The man in the stables?" Delilah poked her head around the pantry door. "Is he a criminal?"

Jess rested his fists on his hips. "He's not convicted of nothing. He was a smuggler. Just like me, Miss Wellesley."

"Not according to your mother, Jess." She settled onto a chair.

"Serve up the soup, Abby. Jess, give a call to your friend to come on to lunch. I stayed in here, Agatha, hoping to avoid that constable. We have crimes enough for him to investigate without giving him even more of an incentive to pop into our pockets."

Delilah wound around Jess' legs, mewling complaints when he opened the back door and gave a shout. She followed him back to the table and planted herself under his chair.

Agatha poured hot water into the teapot then set it on the table and slid onto the chair beside Jess. "Constable Evans doesn't want to investigate our crimes, Aunt Sally. He has no evidence. Just our suspicions, and that is not enough."

"Our crimes?" Aunt Sally sniffed. She took the head of the table, beside her step-niece. She didn't slow down as Jem Webb came quietly into the room. "None of us are guilty of any crimes here, and so we shall maintain. Truth or not, Jess. As your mother said, no charges landed your way, and that constable should not harass you about past misdeeds."

Jem Webb sat down at the far end. "Well, now, Miss Wellesley, I got past misdeeds, and they might be comin' to roost."

"Your shoulders may be broad, Mr. Webb, but I believe we can ensure that no crows will land on you. Do pass the bread, Jess. I am hungry. No, Mr. Webb, do not sneak bread to Samson. He doesn't need it. He needs to be catching mice. I saw one in the cellar this morning."

"Aunt Sally, we might want that constable to concentrate on the arson and the old murder, but he won't. His suspicions will carry more weight than ours do. I do not understand the reason he didn't not ask to speak to Mr. Webb. He knows the man is here. What was he hoping to do? Jess?"

He shrugged as he poured his tea. "Maybe he doesn't want to tip his hand too much. If we've got no reason to fly, we're stuck here until he can get his evidence. Or so he thinks."

Jem Webb shoved his chair back. Samson jumped onto his leg. He bumped his head into the man's chest and mewled. To the surprise of them all, the big man stroked his hand over the marmalade cat's back. Samson purred and draped himself along his leg. "I got to leave." He sounded desperate. "Before that constable comes back with enough evidence to arrest me."

"No, Jem. You stick here. You run, and he'll call that evidence. That will bring trouble down on all of us." Abby Carter shoved a bowl of soup at Jem.

He took it. "I've been down a thorny path before, Mrs. Carter. Ye don't notice the thorns so much after a while."

She handed him a spoon. "Eat up, Jem. You aren't a fool. That's been your one saving grace."

"I didn't think I had any, Mrs. Carter."

"Now you have two. Your smarts and my son's support. Away from Palmer, you might amount to something."

"I've done bad things, Mrs. Carter."

"I'm not your confessor, Jem Webb. Eat your soup before it gets cold." She looked at her son. "We sit tight, and that constable might have wit enough to look around him and ask a few questions. If he does, he'll find more than one person who will talk to him about that Mr. O'Malley. I heard in the shop today that he owes money to several men. Their wives say they're going to be needing that money soon. When Mr. O'Malley doesn't fork it over, his friends will become few on the ground."

"Ye want me to go after O'Malley?" Jem asked quiet.

"No," Agatha said, and Jess said it on the heels of her word.

"Would solve a boatload of trouble."

"Only to make more," Jess said.

"There's that."

"Eat, Jem," Mrs. Carter said again and poured his tea.

"So," Aunt Sally said after she'd had several spoonfuls of soup, "Constable Evans will be sitting at the pub, his ears pricked for information, and he's bound to talk to the vicar. As the vicar talked to O'Malley. The vicar received his information from Richard Helmes. Only the constable will not know that the Rev. Rampling and O'Malley are leagued with your cousin. He will think they are independent sources. Maybe O'Malley does need to be taken care of."

"Aunt Sally," Agatha chided. She shook her head at Jem Webb. "Should we get rid of the vicar next? Where does it stop? It can only stop if it doesn't start."

Jess covered her hand in her lap, squeezed it. "The constable said he would wait. O'Malley's got to be tired of waiting. It's been several months since he tried to get rid of me. With him needing money to repay his debts and the constable not doing anything except listening, O'Malley will get impatient."

"You think he'll do something then?"

"I hope so." He gave a nod to Jem. "We'll be waiting for him."

"You won't plan to go after him, but you'll take care of him if he comes here?"

"It'll be self-defense. Not even that constable would argue with that."

His mother shook her head. "Murder is still wrong, Jess."

"You won't think that if the flames are all around you or he's got his hands around your throat. If he doesn't do anything, then we don't do anything. If he comes after any of us, well, we have to defend ourselves, don't we?"

"That sounds fair," Aunt Sally said. "It's giving him more of a chance than he gave you on the night he burned the steward's cottage. Now, after soup, we've got sweet apples with cream." At the last word, Samson lifted his head and chirped. "Yes, puss, there's cream for you, too."

For a moment, no one spoke, then Jess broke the awkward silence. "Ma, what was in that tea?"

She grinned. "Didn't drink it, did he?"

"What was in it?"

"Dishwater."

After they finished eating, Jess and Jem departed for the stables. Mrs. Carter shooed Agatha and her step-aunt from the kitchen. The cats followed them into the study. She stirred up the fire and turned to find Aunt Sally grinning to herself as she rubbed Samson's forehead. The cat's eyes were closed. He looked on the verge of sleep.

"Aunt Sally, did you put Mrs. Carter up to making the constable's tea with dishwater?"

"Me? Why would I ever think to do that?"

"You did it the last time Cousin Richard was here."

"I thought you had forgotten that. I regret to say that I was guilty of that little plan. I wanted the constable gone. If he's gone, the way Richard soon left, then your Jess won't be in a hurry to leave."

"He said that he plans to stay."

"He's not going off with his friend to the Colonies?"

"He doesn't plan to."

"Plans change."

Chapter 13 ~ Sunday, 12 April

A day passed. Another. Another. Then a fourth. Then a week and more, and still O'Malley kept away from the farm.

The constable rode about, talking to people in the village, on the other farms, on Helmes Farm, but he didn't come to the house.

The vicar preached on the Old Testament story of the handwriting on the wall. The homily was delayed for a christening. Aunt Sally chattered to several ladies as they left the sanctuary. Jess' mother stood outside the bier gate. Mrs. Carter looked to be in full spate, probably exchanging receipts. Her scones were becoming well known. Jess stood beyond, near the pony cart. He talked to a uniformed man.

Agatha drifted into the graveyard. She stared down at little Robert's stony lamb. Aunt Sally's words had haunted her for days. *Plans change.* So many of her own plans had changed. *Would I have been happy with Stanton Myers? Ten years ago he was my whole world.* Yet she had lived quite well without him. She had missed the child she barely met more than she had missed him. *Does that mean I never loved him?*

Without looking at Jess, she could picture every lineament of his features. He had become indispensable to her. She wanted him to make love to her. After New Year's, he hadn't offered to kiss, but many times she had thought him on the verge, especially when he'd been teaching her to punch. He wasn't her whole world, but she wanted him to be in her world permanently. Would she miss him if he disappeared one night? Would she grieve for him if he left with his friend to go to the Colonies?

Would he miss her?

She shook off her megrims and headed for the cart. Aunt Sally joined her. Mrs. Carter reached them as they settled into their seats. Jess clucked to the horse, and the pony cart began rolling back to the farm.

Aunt Sally looked over her shoulder to Agatha. "That was an interesting sermon."

"Nebuchadnezzar?"

"Humble hearts and getting what's due you."

"I didn't see it that way," Agatha said. "You think he was directing it at me, for not listening to Cousin Richard?"

"And for challenging him, God's chosen messenger."

"Just because he's a vicar," Mrs. Carter said, giving Agatha's knee a pat, "doesn't make him God's chosen messenger. There's a difference."

Jess glanced around at his mother, then snapped the reins to gain a little speed from the horse. "Rain's coming."

The first sprinkles dampened them before they reached the farm. The rain started as Jess stopped before the front door and leaped down to help them. He squeezed Agatha's waist as he lifted her off the back-facing seat. Then he helped his mother down.

Mrs. Carter and Aunt Sally bustled in. She watched them enter then looked at Jess, who waited for her. "I saw you speaking with a man while I was in the cemetery. I didn't recognize him."

"Bo Harkness."

"That's not a name from this district. Did my cousin send us another man?"

"No, he's a mate of mine. I contacted him after the constable was here."

"A mate. Like Jem Webb."

"Not quite."

The rain came harder. Jess pushed her toward the door.

They had a late lunch, and during it Aunt Sally realized the cats were missing. "Help me find them," she urged Agatha.

The hunt for the cats took them through every room. In the study, Agatha thought the ledgers on the desk were disarranged, but she couldn't remember how she'd left them. She opened the doors, but found nothing disturbed.

"The cats won't be in drawers," her aunt said.

Agatha shook her head at her worry. In the kitchen Tassie said that she hadn't seen the cats all morning. Mrs. Carter, cleaning up after the lunch, said, "Maybe they went outside."

"They don't like rain. They sense it coming hours before and refuse to go outside."

She found Samson upstairs, hiding under a chair along the gallery. He mewled unhappily and wouldn't come to her arms. He refused to come out from under the chair. "Aunt Sally, what's wrong with him?"

Her step-aunt crossed the landing from the guest wing, where the Carters were roomed. "He was perfectly fine this morning."

"Any sign of Delilah?"

The older woman shook her head, then they heard more meowing. Delilah appeared from the east hall, the family bedchambers. She hissed when she spotted them. Her tail twitched as she approached.

Agatha tried to pick her up, but the calico cat twisted out of her hands and raced to the stairs, pouring down them like water. Samson continued to cry.

"I think he's hurt," Aunt Sally said.

"I can't see anything."

Samson suffered the older woman to run her fingers down his right side, but when she touched his left, he twitched and his ears flattened. He twisted then jumped away. He cried out when he landed and crouched close to the floor. Aunt Sally reached to pick him up.

"Leave him be, Aunt Sally."

"He's hurt."

"Perhaps he jumped and landed wrong."

From the bottom step, Delilah hissed at them.

"If he landed wrong, then it would be his legs, wouldn't it? Tassie will know. She stayed while we were at church, didn't she?"

"She said that she hadn't seen the cats all morning."

"That's a lie," her aunt claimed. "Samson was in the kitchen this morning, begging for cream. Keep a watch on him, Agatha. Samson likes to hide when he's hurt. If he crawls off somewhere and we can't find him—."

For answer, Agatha knelt on the floor. The older woman hurried down the stairs, speaking to Delilah as she passed.

Samson wouldn't come near Agatha, but he didn't leave his spot. Delilah came back up the steps, but she wouldn't let Agatha touch her either. She prowled behind Samson, across the hall and back. She peered between the balcony rails then continued her prowl, meowing constantly.

Sally came back with a saucer of creamy milk. "Tassie says she stayed in the kitchen. She didn't hear anything to do with the cats. Let's see if he'll take this. Here, Samson, some lovely cream." She put the saucer close so he wouldn't have to move.

Delilah stopped and watched. The marmalade cat sniffed, tasted, and lapped it twice. Then he settled his head back onto his front paws. The calico chirped at him. His ears twitched, then he purred, once, a single rumble.

The sound reassured Aunt Sally as little else could. "He will eat, at least. I don't think he is badly hurt."

"Look at Delilah, Aunt Sally. She won't come near me."

Delilah had resumed her rove across the hall and back.

"Something happened while we were gone."

Her aunt bit her bottom lip. "Tassie says not."

"Tassie also said that she hadn't seen the cats this morning."

The women exchanged a look. "I'll check the bedrooms again,"

Aunt Sally offered.

"I'll look around the ground floor. Check the windows and doors."

She toured the rarely used drawing and dining rooms, the oft-used breakfast room and west-facing sitting room. Only her study showed signs of disturbance, if she counted the ledgers that she wasn't certain were disarranged. Her father's farming journal was on top instead of the accounts book. She had looked at the accounts yesterday. The papers on her desk didn't look disarranged. The drawers remained in their disarrangement. The quill in the new inkstand was tilted left instead of right. Little things.

She tried the windows. They were all locked—but hadn't she stood at the terrace window this morning? She had opened it to catch the scent of the hyacinths that had opened only yesterday. *Did I lock the window when I closed it?*

She thought back to the morning: the teacup in her hand, Mrs. Carter singing in the kitchen, the chill breeze. Delilah had heralded Aunt Sally's entrance, prepared for church. Jess followed her in. He had looked dapper in his new bottle green coat and waterfall-tied ascot. Agatha had teased him, and he had grinned as he remarked on her blue dress, "almost the color of your fairy-flower eyes."

"Now that you have complimented each other," Aunt Sally had said drily, "may I have my eggs and toast?"

Laughing, Agatha had closed the window and—no, she couldn't remember if she had latched it or not.

It was latched now.

"What's wrong with Samson?" Jess asked from the door.

"His side's hurt. We thought to leave him where he was until he'll let us pick him up."

He stepped back into the entrance hall to look up at the cat peering over the landing. His gaze tracked along the gallery then dropped to her. "Your aunt's searching the rooms upstairs."

"As I searched the ones down here."

"You think someone came in while we were gone? Samson's side is hurt. Maybe he got kicked when he got in the way."

"Tassie said no one came in."

He crossed to her before he asked, "Have you checked the cash box?"

"It was still locked."

"And you keep the key under the box in the bottom of the left-side drawer. You ain't careful about who sees you get it, Agatha. Check it."

"A thief?"

She didn't question how he knew where she kept the petty cash. She had never tried to hide the cash box or its key when she needed to give him money. Only the large box in her room did she hide. It held the important documents and the pound notes that helped them subsist from quarter to quarter. She opened the top drawer and retrieved the key. It lay in its usual place. From the bottom drawer she took the metal cash box.

The key turned easily. She lifted the lid. "The cash is here."

"Count it."

She counted the bank notes while he skimmed over the coinage.

He told her the amount. "Is that what's supposed to be there?"

"Yes, at least—what I keep here is. The most of what I keep on hand is locked upstairs."

"Check upstairs, Agatha."

"A thief wouldn't pass this by. Mr. Webb—."

"It won't have been Jem. He wouldn't get past Tassie. She don't like him."

"You are saying that she knew someone came into the house? Someone whom she knows and likes?"

"I don't know that. What I'm saying is that Jem doesn't know about the money you keep, here or upstairs. I didn't know about the upstairs box until just now. You need to be more careful about who you announce that to, Agatha. Go check."

Remembering how Delilah had prowled back and forth, as if blocking the way to the family wing, her heart leaped into her throat. "Come with me. If someone came in, they may still be there."

"They'll have scarpered when church was over," he pointed out, yet he followed her up the stairs.

Samson had maneuvered so he could see along the hall and down the steps. He looked up and watched them pass by. Delilah remained on the alert. She raced ahead of them then stopped before Agatha's door. Her tail twitched. When Agatha reached her, Delilah raced into the room and beneath the bed.

"I keep the box in this chest." She opened the big trunk at the foot of the bed. Pushing aside cloth and blankets, she picked up the metal box.

"And the key?"

"In my wardrobe. There's a nail at the backleft corner." She reached in, pushed back the dresses, felt down the corner. She had to bend to reach the nail. The key hung from its ribbon, still in place. When she emerged, Jess was shaking his head.

"You need better hiding places."

"The key is hidden. The box is hidden."

"Not from a serious search. Neither of these boxes actually need a key. I could jimmy the lock. Or drop them from a few feet, and they would bust open."

Agatha opened the box and stared at the contents. Or the lack of them.

"What is it?"

"It's empty." She swallowed.

He picked up the box and lifted her up at the same time. "Quite empty. What did you keep in here?"

"The deed to the farm and my father's will."

"Where do you keep the money?"

She walked to the hearth. She pressed the smooth paneled wall beside the mantel. The wood creaked then sprang open. She reached in and withdrew a leather wallet. She opened it—and breathed an audible sigh of relief. "The money's still here."

"All of it?"

She did a quick count. "Yes."

"So, all that was stolen were the papers that prove the farm belongs to you."

She put the money back and pressed the panel shut. "You think my cousin—. But he isn't here. How would taking the documents help him?"

"Would he know about this box? That you keep the deed and the will here?"

She shook her head 'no'. "But what good would the deed do him? Everyone knows the farm is mine. I am listed as the only legal holder of Helmes Farm and Helmes House in the manorial rolls."

"The vicar didn't know that, did he? Did Lord Chalmesley ever see these papers?"

"Yes, for he came here for Probate, after my father's death, and then again for my mother and my stepfather. The lawyer read my father's will bequeathing the house and farm to me. My mother had little personal property to dispose of beside her jewels, but my stepfather left his farm to Aunt Sally."

"So, his lordship and your lawyer can attest in court that the property is yours. Stealing the will and the deed will not do Helmes any good."

"But my cousin is in Ipswich."

"While his man O'Malley is here. I need to find O'Malley."

"But how did he know about this box? He never came above stairs."

"Did Dick Helmes know about it?"

"Well—yes."

"He's the source. He will have told O'Malley what to look for. He probably was hoping your money was in this box as well." Jess jigged the box enough to let the lid slam shut. He released her arm then handed the box to her. "Find a better place for this box. And for that key. Bank the majority of that money, Agatha. You were lucky. You should keep only a few pounds in the house."

"Yes, point my folly out to me."

He touched her cheek. "Very little folly. The money was well hidden. I'll get the deed and the will back for you."

"You think O'Malley came in, looking for money as well as these documents? Yet why did he not take what was in the petty cash box? And why would Tassie let him in the house so he could rob me?"

"Maybe she didn't know he was going to rob you. Maybe she didn't care. Doesn't matter. I will get those documents back. If we can catch him."

"You and ... Jem Webb?"

"Me and Jem, yes."

.~.~.~.

The rain was steady and cold. Jess bent his head and plowed through the steady drops to the stable. But Jem wasn't there, only Little Mike, sitting on a stack of hay and whistling as he used a small knife to nick shavings off a stick of wood.

"Little Mike, where's Big Jem?"

The boy looked up from his whittling. "He's out on Big Clive. He left afore ye got back from church."

Jess reached for a headstall and headed for the other Suffolk Punch, a raw-boned gelding that like to fight the bit. Yet Ollie would run fast and keep the pace.

He entered the horse's stall. Ollie eyed him but took the bit and accepted the headstall. Jess led him out, tied the reins to the latch on the half-door and headed for a saddle. He threw another question at Little Mike. "Did Jem say anything about where he was heading?"

"Ol' Denny talked to him, not me."

"Where is Denny?"

"He said rain's the time for fishing, so off he went."

Jess swung a blanket and then a saddle onto Ollie. The horse shook himself, and Jess checked the girth strap again. He pulled Ollie into the rain before he swung up. "Does Denny have a favorite fishing spot?"

"By the bridge, the one you cross to go to Wellesley Farm, over past the wood."

Ollie didn't like the rain, but once he realized Jess was determined, the big Punch put his head down and galloped over the fields. They covered the ground to the river quickly, and Jess turned his head for the bridge that crossed to the neighboring farm.

He found the old man exactly as the boy had said, fishing on the lee side of the stone bridge. Denny watched as he rode close. He pulled in his fishing line and set his pole to the side as Jess dismounted and led Ollie closer. He pulled his pipe from his mouth. "Wondered how long it would take ye."

"You saw Jem Webb?"

"I did."

"What did he say to you? Come on, Denny," he added, when the man reached for his fishing pole and swung the line back into the water. "Miss Helmes is missing some important documents, the deed for the farm and her father's will. What did Webb say to you?"

Denny's eyebrows rose. "No money?"

"No. She hid that better than she hid the documents."

"Strange that they'd take the documents."

Ollie took that moment to toss his head and pulled back on the reins. Jess hauled the horse's head down then gave the glare he'd been controlling to the old man. "If they wanted to cause her trouble with a claim on the farm, they would need those documents."

"Aye."

"Denny, what did Webb say?"

"He saw a man go into the house while you were gone. He was going to follow him."

"Did he say who the man was? Was it O'Malley?"

"Funny ye should guess that."

"Was it?"

"Yea, it was O'Malley. Why'd ye guess him?"

"Because O'Malley's working with Dick Helmes to get the farm from Agatha."

The old man lifted his line from the water. He looked around with narrowed eyes. "Agatha, is it? She been givin' ye more than house-room?"

"House-room is all," he said tersely. "She's a lady. I'm just a rough laborer."

"Bit more than that, I'd say."

"Did Webb follow O'Malley?"

"He didn't have to. O'Malley never left the house."

"Never left—." Water trickled under his collar and began streaking down his spine.

"Not that Webb saw." He tossed his line in the water again.

"He never left the house? Then where did Webb go?"

"That constable showed up. He wanted Webb to go back to the village with him."

Jess didn't believe him. "Jem Webb wouldn't go tamely with that constable."

"An' so he didn't. He knocked him down, jumped on the horse, and hared off."

"What did the constable do?"

"Got up, dusted off, climbed back on his horse, and headed back to the village."

"So Webb's left." And O'Malley remained in the house, hidden somewhere. He had kicked the cat, stolen the documents, and waited for his opportunity to—do what? Assault Agatha again? With Jess was miles away.

"An' good riddance to Webb. He ain't for farm-work. Don't care that he's yer mate."

"Why didn't Little Mike tell me this?"

"I told 'em not to."

Jess swung back on Ollie's back. "You may not like Jem Webb, but Miss Helmes' farm papers are missing. O'Malley's got them somewhere. He's probably looking for a chance to steal what money Miss Helmes has. That constable will be heading back here with men to track Webb. And you sit here fishing. Denny, I thought you cared what happened to Miss Helmes. You may not like me, but don't throw her into ruination."

The old man squinted up through the rain. "Got nothin' 'gainst ye. Don't care for that bruiser yer brought in, Carter, an' that's fact."

"So you'll side with her cousin and not her because of Jem Webb."

"I'm not taking sides."

"If you're not helping her, you're helping her cousin. But keep fishing. I'm sure trout for supper is more to your taste."

Jess wheeled the horse and set him galloping back. How much time had he lost going after Denny to find out where Jem had gone? How much time before O'Malley decided he would wait no longer and make his move? Had the man hidden in Agatha's room? He remembered how Delilah had raced under the bed. The calico surely wouldn't hide where O'Malley was hiding. There was nowhere else to hide in Agatha's room. So O'Malley wouldn't have seen her hiding place for her money. That should remain safe.

But where was O'Malley hiding?

Dusk was falling as he rode up to the house. Lights blazed from the windows. He saw movement in a downstairs window. Everything looked safe.

And he was soaked to the skin.

He bent low as Ollie rode into the stable's shelter. He dropped off and began unsaddling the horse. Then he saw Big Clive in his stall. Jess hesitated then asked softly into the stable's darkness, "Jem? You there?"

"Back here."

He took the steps needed to let darkness cloak him as well. "You've got trouble with that constable now."

From the darkest corner came "Ye know it. I'll be needin' to get gone, Carter."

"I've got coin I can give you."

"I won't lie; I need it. Ye give me a chance I didn't expect. I'll remember that."

"When will you leave?"

A rustling. A blacker shadow against the wall. "After we take care of O'Malley. Denny tell ye that?"

"Where is O'Malley?"

"Not where I looked fer 'im. I reckon he's still in the house."

"Still in—surely that's not possible. Agatha and her aunt searched the place looking for the cats."

"Neither of them ladies has ever crossed the law an' had to hide. Trust me, he's still in there. Waitin' fer dark, an' I'm waitin' fer him."

Remembering Agatha's idea of a hiding place, he had to agree with Jem. He groaned. The house would have dozens more hiding places. The ladies had not even climbed to the second floor and the attics. "You got more of a plan than jump out and knock him on the head?"

Jem chuckled, the sound as dark as his corner. "A bit more than that. An' when that constable comes back, ye give him O'Malley in place of me, an' that gets me farther on the road to Liverpool."

"Still heading for Canada?"

"Still am. Company's welcome."

"I'm sticking here. Dick Helmes is turning out to be a piece of work."

"Ye gonna make an honest woman of her?"

"She don't need me to do that."

"Gossip's been flyin'. It'd take a blind man not to see the sparks between ye two."

"I ain't taking love advice from you, Jem."

He laughed. "I'm the last one to give it. Go on to the house. They'll be wonderin' what's keepin' ye. I'll take care of Ollie."

Jess protested, but Jem pointed out that he'd spent long enough talking that it would seem that he'd dried and curried the horse himself. No one would see Jem working inside the stable.

Tassie remained in the kitchen. She ignored him as usual. His mother clucked at his soaked state then said supper would be late.

"Where are the ladies?"

"In the study. Jess! You need to change."

"Yeah," he agreed, but he headed for the study. He shut the door and took a good look around to make sure O'Malley didn't have a hiding place in the room. Then he steamed in front of the fire as he told them about Jem Webb and the constable. "Webb is gone," he lied.

Delilah came to him. She avoided his dripping clothes but sat herself nearby. She began licking her paw. "How's Samson?" he asked.

"He's retreated to his chair on the landing," Aunt Sally said. "But he drank all his cream, and he's not crying so much."

Agatha stared at him. She seemed bursting with questions, but he gave her a steady look. She looked down at her hands. "Your mother is holding supper. You will need to change. It's not wise to stay in wet clothes."

"Aye, I'm on my way upstairs."

He gave a cursory look around his room, but he didn't want to alert O'Malley that he was watched for. Samson mewed as he passed on his way back downstairs. Jess bent and chucked the cat under the chin. Samson flicked his tail but refused to emerge from under the chair. And Jess thought he heard a creak. But that could be the wind blowing. The rain was harder now, the house itself colder, as if the stiff wind sucked all its warmth. He gave one glance down the east hall, where the family bedchambers were, then trotted downstairs.

Tassie had left by then. They gathered around the kitchen table for soup and butter-laden baked potatoes, a wedge of farm cheese and scones, finished off with hot tea and cream.

Aunt Sally offered to help his mother with the dishes. Jess intended to make a good search of the ground floor rooms. He reckoned O'Malley was on the first floor. He wanted to flush the man out—and he needed to leave a door unlocked so Jem could get inside.

But Agatha snared his sleeve when he headed for the drawing room. "We need to talk."

"We don't have time," he whispered. "Not now. Just—be careful. Jem thinks O'Malley is still in the house."

"Still in the house?" Her voice spiraled up.

He dragged her into her study to keep from alerting the entire house. "Hush. We're going to set a trap."

"A trap?" she repeated, like an idiot.

He nodded. "Keep quiet about it. We'll go about our evening like usual. He'll be waiting for his best opportunity, probably to force you to tell him where your money is kept. Then we'll get him."

Chapter 14 ~ Sunday, 12 April

They stayed up late, but O'Malley didn't stir from his hidey-hole. He definitely wasn't in the occupied bedchambers, but it was a large house with several more bedchambers on the first floor and even more on the second floor. The old servants' rooms were on the half-floor beneath the attic.

Trying to predict when O'Malley would strike was another impossibility. Since he was still working for Dick Helmes, Jess reckoned that the former steward would not torch Helmes House the way he had the cottage. The quarter-payment kept in the hidden cache in Agatha's room would not be the man's only target. He would be after Agatha, for firing him when he made advances. He would want to get his own back on Jess, who had supplanted him.

Agatha didn't like Jess' logic, but she couldn't argue with it.

Jem Webb slunk into the house via the terrace door in the study. He sat before the fire, soaking up the heat. Aunt Sally had fussed over him, but it was Delilah, leaping into his lap, that surprised them all.

"There," Aunt Sally said. "I knew you were a good man. Delilah's just confirmed it."

Jem shook his head. Mrs. Carter pressed another cup of tea on him. He accepted it and drank it quietly.

Agatha argued for the trap to be set in Jess' bedchamber.

He shook his head. "No. He'll be going into yours. He knows you have to keep the money there. It's the old lord's chamber. He'll be expecting there to be a secret hiding place, and he'll need to force it out of you. Jem will wait in my chamber."

"Aye," the big man agreed. "Besides, Miss Helmes, he's after ye personally. Rape's an ugly word, but I'll say it." He looked her squarely in the eye. Under his stroking hand, Delilah purred. "His hate fer Jess is because ye fired 'im. He ain't done nothing else because yer hard to get to. But this morning he found a way in. No tellin' how long he's been connin' that Tassie, but he did. He's waitin' somewhere, an' he wants what ye denied 'im all those months ago."

She had folded her arms protectively as he talked. "How can you be certain?"

"That's the way I'd do it. That's how he thinks."

And that set her insides to quavering.

She felt awkward preparing for bed knowing that Jess was stationed behind the heavy curtains over the tall windows. She pulled the bed curtains against the night's chill and crawled through them onto the mattress.

Only to stick her head back out. "Jess. What if this doesn't work? What if Mr. Webb is wrong?"

"He's not wrong."

She'd thought Webb's excuse weak, but Jess had accepted it. "You're that sure?"

"If we're wrong and he goes into my chamber, Jem'll handle it. If we're right and he comes in here, I'll keep you safe. He's got no other reason to stay in the house hidden. Now blow out the candle and pretend to sleep."

Delilah mewed from the floor. Agatha let the cat jump onto the bed then wet her fingers to snuff the candle.

The complete dark gave her shivers. She pulled the covers to her chin.

Mrs. Carter had a pallet in Aunt Sally's room, and Aunt Sally had her little one-shot pistol. She had bragged that she could drill a hole in the pips of a playing card.

The words reminded Agatha of Stanton's death. She'd cast that vagrant thought aside as they had discussed their plans. Now it returned to haunt her.

What if Cousin Richard hadn't murdered Stanton? What if someone else had done so? Her stepfather. Or Aunt Sally.

No, neither of them would have done it. They would never break a commandment and English law.

But Agatha remembered how Robbie Wellesley had seethed when Aunt Sally guessed at her pregnancy and Agatha had had to admit that Stanton knew, that he had known for days and days, and that he had shown no sign of proposing marriage.

Aunt Sally had seethed hotter than her stepfather. She had thrown a prized vase when Agatha declared that she wouldn't have Stanton forced to marry her. Her step-aunt had ranted that a man couldn't treat her like his doxy.

A woman could shoot a hole in a man's skull as easily as a man could. Aunt Sally had the necessary anger and resolve to defend her niece from a young rake turning her into his fancy piece.

Stanton would not have anticipated danger from the older woman. From Robbie Wellesley, yes. Her stepfather had shouted when he'd spoken to the young man the last time he'd come to the house. That was long before Aunt Sally revealed Agatha's pregnancy.

For that matter, Stanton would not have suspected her. He thought her his gullible fool, right up to the night she demanded he propose or leave.

When he was missing the next day, she thought he'd landed on the wrong side of her ultimatum. Her stepfather had said, "Good riddance." She couldn't remember what Aunt Sally had said, merely that she'd stood firm as a rock all through the pregnancy and the stillbirth and Agatha's grief for a child that had never had a chance to breathe life.

Agatha tossed onto her side. Delilah groused then settled over her feet.

Her hatred of Stanton had grown with the babe in her womb then died like ashes within weeks of putting the babe in the ground. She took Robbie Wellesley's stance never to be ashamed of loving, and she found strength in keeping her head high as the gossip flooded the village and the district.

No one had ever said anything more to her about Stanton Myers. He might never have lived. The villagers' lips only loosened with the finding of his corpse.

"Jess?"

"You're supposed to pretend to be asleep."

"I can't sleep."

"Worried?"

"No." She sat up. She might as well admit to what was truly bothering her. She pushed back the bed curtain on the window-side. The dying fire cast off a little light so the room was not as pitch-dark as it had seemed. "What have you heard about me? About the baby I had?"

He huffed. A whisper of sound, then she saw him crossing to her from the window. She pushed the curtain back some more and sat up, dangling her bare feet over the mattress.

Delilah chuffed and jumped off the bed.

He loomed over her, a darker shadow. "A young lady who got herself into trouble."

"That wouldn't have been all they said. I'm sure a few were happy to tell you that and more."

"An uppity young lady who tangled with a rake and came off the worse. Got herself a babe. Lucky it died." Even in hushed tones, the words cut.

"That's cruel."

"He regretted it."

His voice had a glut of smug satisfaction. "Did you plant him a facer?"

"I did." He sat beside her. The dip of the mattress dropped her against him. He touched her knee then quickly removed his hand. "I don't judge you, Agatha. My ma doesn't. People make mistakes. Like me and smuggling."

She scooted a half-inch closer until they were hip-to-hip. The darkness made her brave, but she could still only manage hushed words. "I keep remembering how you kissed me at New Year's."

He drew a sharp breath. "You keep remembering that, too?"

She bobbed her head although he couldn't see it. "I wonder why you never—I'm older than you, and I'm not untouched, and—."

"That's not the reason."

"Then why?"

"You're my boss. And better than me. More than just you're gentry and I'm a laborer. You've got a fine education and fine ideals and—."

"Jess, those don't matter."

From across the room, Delilah hissed.

He squeezed her knee then slipped off the bed.

Agatha quickly lay down as she heard the doorknob slowly turn. If she hadn't been awake, if the cat hadn't warned them, she doubted she would have heard that stealthy sound.

The door opened. The lamp in the hallway had been extinguished.

The door shut.

The faintest sounds tracked the intruder across the room. The bed curtains were thrust back.

Agatha sat up.

A hand reached in and grabbed her hair and jerked. She cried out.

Then the fingers were torn from her hair. She heard punches thudding into flesh.

Agatha scrambled out of bed and raced to the fireplace to light a candle. The sudden flare of light revealed Jess and O'Malley fighting. Gold flashed on metal. The Irishman had a knife.

She screamed a warning and ran for the door. It bounced back on its hinges, and she barely slid out of way when Jem Webb barreled past her, heading for the fight. He grabbed the hand holding the knife and began twisting it.

O'Malley screamed and kicked. Jess hit him hard in the face then in the stomach. The two men forced the former steward down to the floor.

The light level increased. Agatha saw Mrs. Carter standing in the doorway with a lamp, and behind her was Aunt Sally.

Jem Webb hauled O'Malley up from the floor and thrust him into a chair. Jess stood before him, fists clenched. He didn't wipe the blood on his mouth and chin.

Aunt Sally came up beside Agatha. She held her little pistol before her.

Mrs. Carter set down her lamp and went to light another one.

"Well? What are you doing here?" Jess demanded.

O'Malley cursed. Webb gave him a hard buffet then straightened the man in the chair. He began a rough search, jerking open the man's coat. From an inner pocket he produced a gun which he handed to Jess. Jess stared at it then glanced at the knife on the floor. "If the knife was for Miss Helmes, who was the gun for? Me?"

The Irishman clamped his mouth shut.

Jem Webb found a fat pouch of coins and a slim leather wallet. But the wallet held only a single sheet of paper. He tossed the pouch to Agatha. She barely caught it. The wallet he handed to Jess who handed the paper to Agatha.

"Where's the deed, O'Malley? And the will?"

He grinned and spat blood. "Where you'll have a hard time finding them."

Agatha looked up from the paper. "My cousin Richard wrote this. He says you are to take the will and the deed and any money you can find in the house." She hefted the pouch. "I suppose this is the money he paid you."

He glared at her. His hands clenched into fists, but he kept them on his knees.

"You are working for my cousin Richard Helmes. You have been all along."

When O'Malley just stared, Webb smacked his head again. "Answer the lady."

He slewed his head around to look up at the big man. "I'm working for Helmes. Just like you. And you." He glared at Jess. "He sent you to keep watch on the farm. You're poaching on his preserves, Carter. You're supposed to work for him, not be spooning with his cousin and making plans to step into his boots."

Agatha strangled a cry of outrage, for Webb had smacked him again.

"What was this tonight? Ye came in here. Ye grabbed her. What were ye plannin'?"

He spat again then grinned, revealing bloody teeth. "A little playtime for me. He'd never know. It's not like she's a virgin. She gave it up years ago."

Jess stepped forward and hit him hard. Jem caught the chair and set it back on its four legs. O'Malley, blood streaming from his nose, cursed them all. He wiped at the blood. "You done broke my nose."

"Miss Helmes is a lady," Jem said. "Ye'll keep yer trap shut on aught else."

"You stole the deed and the will. Why?"

He didn't look at Jess. He glared at Agatha. "If she don't have them, Helmes can make his claim."

"That won't work," Agatha protested. Aunt Sally put her arm around her shoulders. "Lord Chalmesley knows what's in the will and the deed. The deed is recorded in the manorial rolls."

"Happen his lordship will support your cousin since you've been cavorting with Carter here."

Jem hit him cold, a hard whack that knocked his head over. When O'Malley managed to right his head on his neck, the bruiser said, "I warned ye. Watch yer mouth."

O'Malley craned his head as if his neck hurt. "I just told you the plan."

"What do you get out of it?" Jess asked.

He grinned again, foolish when both men were ready to hit him. "A quick tumble to teach her a lesson and that money. I'd have enjoyed it, too, teaching her that lesson."

Jem hit him again.

"Enough," Jess said. "We won't get no more out of him up here. Let's get him down to the cellar. The constable can pick him up in the morning."

O'Malley surged out of the chair. He plowed into Jess, knocking him back, then he came round with a knife and stabbed at Jem.

The pistol fired.

A hole blossomed on his temple. Momentum checked, he stared at them. The knife clattered to the floor. Then O'Malley crumpled.

Jem dropped to his knees. Aunt Sally said, "Don't bother. He's dead."

For the third time in her life, Agatha swooned.

.~.~.~.

Jess caught her. He scooped her up. Looking around, he strode over to lay her on the bed.

Behind him, Jem said, "That's torn it."

"Whyever so?" Aunt Sally said, her sangfroid unchanged.

His mother bustled over and scooted him out of the way. She patted Agatha's cheeks. Jess turned to the older woman. "We needed his testimony against her cousin. And we still don't know where he hid those documents."

She bent and picked up the letter that Agatha had dropped. "Should we put this back in his pocket?"

Jess thought swiftly. "No. It raises too many other questions. We'll keep it simple for that constable. Nothing about our trap, nothing about O'Malley working for her cousin—and nothing about Jem."

"Oh, yes, I had forgotten that little complication." She looked down at O'Malley. She neither looked nor sounded repentant. "We shall just have to wrest the location of the documents from Richard when he comes. H he is certain to come now, with his henchman dead."

Jem stared at the body then looked at Jess. He was holding his forearm. A red stain was spreading under his hand. "This wasn't in the plan."

"We'll weather it, mate. He hurt Agatha, we're both bleeding—."

"I'm not hurt," she said faintly.

Jess turned and saw his mother supporting her. Her eyes were on the man on the floor, but they lifted to him. "He is dead, isn't he?"

"Your aunt don't miss, it seems."

Her bruised gaze transferred to Aunt Sally.

The older woman's cool faltered. She covered it with quick words. "Well, we can't leave him lying on the floor. Where shall we put him?"

Jess bit his lip. "I'll fetch Denny and send for the constable."

"No," his ma said. "I'll fetch Denny. You take Agatha out of here, to your room is best, I think. Sally, you want to practice your needle skills on that gash on Jem's arm?" She left on those words.

"But what will we tell Constable Evans?" Agatha asked as he lifted her from the bed.

"The truth. He came for you and got stopped."

"By me," Jem said.

"No," Aunt Sally said, "by me. It is, after all, my pistol. Look at you. You are bleeding all over the place. Come with me."

Jem looked at the body, looked at Aunt Sally, then nodded at Jess and followed her out.

"He is truly dead?" Agatha asked faintly.

"Here, now, you're not going to swoon again."

"I thought you said I didn't swoon."

"Here and there and back again." He turned toward the door.

"I can walk."

"Let's not risk that just yet."

"I can't believe—He was truly in the house, waiting, watching, all day."

"We got lucky."

She shivered and tucked her head against his shoulder. "She just shot him."

*Dangerous territory*, Jess thought, *since that was the way Stanton Myers had died.* Yet all he allowed was "Aye," and he kept walking to the west hall. He set her down to open the door then lifted her again.

His bedroom lamp was still lit.

"You shouldn't carry me. You're hurt. Jem's hurt. He's hurt bad."

"He'll never admit it." He placed her on his bed then sat down on the mattress.

She stayed in a sitting position. Her hands clutched his shirt. "He can't just up and leave, not when he's hurt like that. You can't let him. He needs to stay until he's healed."

"I don't think anyone can tell Jem what to do or keep him from it. If he's set on doing something, he will. That constable will be here before long. He's after Jem, Agatha. They had a dust-up while we were at church. Evans came to arrest him. Jem won't stand still for that to happen."

"Unless we can hide him."

"We'll think of something." He searched her scalp. "Did he hurt you?" He felt along her neck. "He grabbed you hard and jerked. I thought he'd snap your neck."

"You saved me." Those periwinkle eyes were steady on his. "You've been saving me all along."

"And bringing you trouble. That burned cottage. The trouble with Jem."

"I would have had to face O'Malley on my own if you hadn't come." She gripped his hand where it still cupped her neck. "I will have to face my cousin on my own if you aren't here."

His mouth twisted. "Your cousin sent me. O'Malley spoke true. I was working for your cousin when I came here."

"But you didn't keep working for him. If you had been, you wouldn't have stopped O'Malley's assault on me that first day. If you had been, you wouldn't have worked so hard on the farm. I needed you, Jess, and you stepped up."

"I lied to you, Agatha."

"When? You told me from the first that my cousin sent you."

"He sent me to spy. He sent me to keep this place for him, not for you. He sent me to make sure O'Malley didn't touch you. I've brought you trouble. You need a better man than me."

Her fingers covered his mouth. "I don't need a better man. I don't want a better man. I want you."

"God, Agatha." He bent his head to the crook of her neck. "Thank God. I want you so much." He lifted his head and skimmed his lips, still sore, still bleeding, along her cheek to her mouth. Against her lips he said, "I need you, only you."

He kissed her. He denied himself for weeks and weeks. It was as good as the New Year's kiss. Better. Even with his lip hurting. Her response fired him, and he bore her back to the mattress. She giggled and gave him kiss for kiss, her response growing as ardent as his.

Someone cleared their throat to interrupt them.

"That constable will be here before long," his ma said. "We need to get ready for him."

Yet she had a smile for him. When Agatha hugged her, she beamed and returned the hug. Then she exclaimed, "Look at you. He's got you all bloody. Jess, go wash your face in my room. Come here, young lady. We need to clean you up and get you dressed for company."

Chapter 15 ~ Monday, 13 April

"I say," Abby Carter said, "that nobody cleans him up. I've covered him with a sheet, but we don't do nothing more. Let the constable do it."

"We have to hide Jem," Agatha said. "He's not fit for traveling."

"Indeed he's not," Aunt Sally agreed. "He lost more blood than he'll admit to. He can stay in my room. That constable will not dare look in my room."

"Tassie will be coming."

"Leave her to me, Agatha. I'll keep her busy in the kitchen with me."

"And what do we tell Constable Evans?" Agatha asked. "That's Jem's blood on the floor as well as—as well as O'Malley's. How do we explain that? Unless we can wrap some of the bloody cloths you used on Jess. We could pretend Jess is hurt."

"That will work." Her step-aunt had not hesitated once since she'd come into Agatha's room during the fighting. "And we will tell the truth, all but Jem's part. I shot O'Malley. To save Jess, who was fighting a man with a knife. A man who broke in here to do unspeakable things to you. Your neck's bruising nicely. Keep it uncovered. It supports our story."

"Evidence," Jess said. "The constable will have his evidence." Then he went off with Aunt Sally. Mrs. Carter headed downstairs to control anyone who might come in through the kitchen.

Agatha caught a glimpse of herself in the mirror. Blood smeared her face. Jess' blood. Her hair was flyaway from being ripped at. Her neck hurt. Her nightgown was torn at the neck. She reached up and deliberately tore it more. She didn't want to wear that garment ever again. Then she went to fetch a plain gown.

She tried not to look at the covered body on the floor. She used her step-aunt's chamber to wash and then change into the chemise and dull brown gown. She washed her face then rebraided her hair. The woman looking back at her from the mirror wasn't a stranger, but she felt much better than she looked. Good. Constable Evans would have more evidence.

Downstairs, she lit all of the lamps. She perched on the straight-backed chair in the hall and waited. Dealing with the constable felt like boring necessity—but much preferable to the moment when she'd seen O'Malley's knife flashing for Jess.

Voices. Agatha looked and saw Jess descending the stair ahead of Aunt Sally. His arm, wrapped in bloody bandages, rested in a sling. Not all the blood had been wiped from his chin. His swollen lip looked ready to burst open again.

"We're not waiting in the hall for him, surely?" Aunt Sally protested.

Jess took Agatha's arm and towed her up. "No, we aren't. The study will do us. Miss Wellesley, will you carry a lamp in?"

Agatha dragged her feet rather than follow her step-aunt. "It seems wrong, somehow, to plan to lie to a representative of the law."

"We're telling the truth, Agatha. O'Malley attacked you. He stole important documents from you. He was after money."

"We're omitting a good part of the truth, Jess. That's wrong."

"I owe Jem. He's been my mate. I won't turn him over to that constable."

She could not argue against his loyalty. Not when she still saw that knife flashing around before Aunt Sally had shot O'Malley.

Mrs. Carter carried in hot tea. "Drink it down. Look at you, Agatha. You need to be over by the fire. You're still shivering. Jess, add a splash of whiskey to her tea. All of you, drink some of it. It will steady you. I'll have scones ready before that constable arrives."

The hall clock ticked away. It chimed the half-hour.

Finally they heard thundering hoofbeats, the constable coming quickly when it was much too late to have saved anyone from Reece O'Malley.

Jess went to the door. The ladies trailed behind him. He stood in the opening. The cold night tried to come in around him.

"Aye," Jess said. "Come in."

Aunt Sally wrapped an arm around Agatha's waist.

Jess shifted aside, and Constable Evans walked in. "You sent for me, Miss Helmes?" His eyes narrowed on her before returning to Jess. "The boy said there had been a fight. Did Jem Webb come back?"

"Jem Webb's not here," Jess said. "We got another problem."

"Another problem?"

"Mr. O'Malley got into the house. He attacked Miss Helmes."

The constable looked at her. His eyes narrowed. "You fought him off? You fought him, Mr. Carter?"

"He pulled a knife," Jess started.

"And I shot him," Aunt Sally interjected. "His body is upstairs on the floor of my niece's bed chamber. We left him where he fell."

Evans drew a deep breath. "Upstairs? May I—?"

"I'll take you up," Jess offered.

"No," Agatha said. "He cut you with that knife." She stepped away from Aunt Sally. "I'll escort the constable upstairs."

"Hush, both of you. The constable is my responsibility. You go sit down before a fire, Agatha. You are as cold as ice. Have Mrs. Carter serve more tea. Constable Evans will want some as well, I am certain. Not dishwater this time."

He raised his brows then followed the older woman up the stairs. She carried a lamp from the gallery into the chamber.

The upstairs was silent for a long time.

Jess urged Agatha into the study. Mrs. Carter was pressing a cup of sugared tea into her hands when the constable and Aunt Sally returned. Her step-aunt trailed behind the man. She looked paler than he. Mrs. Carter brushed past him without acknowledging him, but she had set an extra teacup and saucer on the tray.

"Please sit down, Constable Evans."

He perched on a straight-backed chair and accepted the tea. He stared into the liquid then glanced up. "She gave me dishwater last time?"

"You offended her."

"I will endeavor not to do so in the future. My men will remove Mr. O'Malley, if you can furnish a cart to transport him to the village. You look a little better, Miss Helmes. Not so shaky. And you, Mr. Carter. Your color is good, as well. No shock."

Agatha wanted his attention on her, not on Jess. "I have been terrified and horrified this night, Constable, but I will try to be a good witness for you."

"Thank you, Miss Helmes. If I might question you alone—."

She had feared this, but if she stuck to the truth, omitting only the trap and Jem Webb, her story would tally with Jess' and Aunt Sally's.

"I will wait in the kitchen," Aunt Sally sniffed.

"I'd rather not leave," Jess said. "Miss Helmes fainted earlier. She's been mauled and seen fighting and watched a man get shot and die. I'd rather not leave."

"I will be fine, Mr. Carter. I will remain in this chair. The constable is not going to attack me."

Jess scowled. "As you wish, Miss Helmes. I'll send for a cart. You need me, I'll be just in the hall, waiting." He strode out with more energy than he should have used, since he was supposed to have lost all that extra blood in her bedchamber and on the gallery carpet.

Constable Evans pulled out a folded paper and a pencil. "May I record your statement, Miss Helmes? Would you tell me what happened, from the beginning?"

"I—would rather not, but I understand your need for evidence. I was asleep. Something woke me. I am not certain what it was. Perhaps a sound. I do remember that Delilah, my aunt's cat, the calico one—she started hissing. I couldn't see anything. Then a hand grabbed me—."

"You had no candle or lamp in the room?"

"Nothing lit. I was sleeping. I only had the light from the hearthfire."

"There is a candle now. It has burned low."

"I lit it—after—after the gun shot." Her first lie. Would he ask Jess and Aunt Sally when she lit that candle? They wouldn't be prepared for that question.

"So someone grabbed you?"

"I screamed. And O'Malley—."

"You recognized your assailant? I thought it was too dark to see."

"He spoke to me. He said—he said what he wanted to do to me." Another lie, but this one neither Jess nor Aunt Sally would have to know about. "I do not wish to repeat those words." And her shudder was not wholly faked.

He grunted. "Go on."

"O'Malley covered my mouth and told me not to scream. He said that he had a knife." *O'Malley did have a knife. I'm not embellishing.* "I was afraid. He tore my nightrail. I couldn't—I couldn't just let him—so I screamed again."

"He would not have liked that. You were brave to do it."

"He tried to choke me then."

"And that scream is the one that brought in Mr. Carter? Your aunt's room was closer, but she tells me that she came in after Mr. Carter was already fighting Mr. O'Malley."

She stared. "Is that a question?" *Do I make up an answer?* "I don't know why Jess—Mr. Carter arrived in my room before Aunt Sally did. I was fighting for my life, Constable Evans. All I know is that Jess— Mr. Carter got O'Malley off me. I lit the candle; I thought light would help. I saw O'Malley's knife. Did you find it?"

"I did. When did your aunt come in?"

"I don't know. She was just there with her little pistol. They kept fighting and—then they were apart. O'Malley raised his knife and lunged—. And Aunt Sally shot him." *There. All told. Only two lies.* And those lies she would never deny.

He wrote several lines then looked from under his eyebrows. "O'Malley never gave another reason for being in your room?"

Agatha did not have to fake a shudder. "He said very little to me, constable. Just what I told you."

"Did you search his pockets?"

She shook her head, aware of her hair shifting loose over her shoulders. She saw his gaze flicker. "You mean, after he was dead? I didn't want to go near him."

"He had no wallet or money pouch."

"You think we'd steal a dead man's wallet?"

"I didn't say that. I find it curious that he had no wallet."

"You do know that Mr. O'Malley has been without work since I fired him in early December? I do not believe he ever looked for work. I do not know the reason that he lingered in Helmesford, except that my cousin may have paid him to remain."

"You bring up your cousin again, Miss Helmes?"

"O'Malley was his man before he worked for me. He made numerous comments that his first loyalty was owed to my cousin."

"He told you this last night?"

She sighed out a deep breath and held on to her patience. "No. I told you what he said to me last night. The other comments were throughout his employ and on the day I fired him."

"Do you still believe he burned the steward's cottage?"

"I believe tonight is proof he bore me a grudge. Is tonight's attack acceptable evidence to you?"

Her facetious tone earned a sharp look. "I did take statements from several of your farm workers and some others in the village. Most of them attested that O'Malley could bear a grudge for a long time. A few hinted that he was violent, but they wouldn't swear to it. Still others swore that he was a good man, fired unjustly, a man who was trusted by your cousin."

"That last comment sounds like the vicar. He is good friends with my cousin. He believes everything my cousin writes to him."

He checked his notes, but he didn't confirm her guess. He merely put a mark of some sort on a previous page then flipped back to his current page.

"What conclusion did you reach about O'Malley, constable?"

His brow contracted a little. "He demands others pay for his pints, but that has nothing to do with committing arson. I picked up a couple of rumors that he'd gotten two farm girls with babies. Tonight's attack on you, I will have to take into consideration. I would speak with Miss Wellesley next, Miss Helmes. If you would send her in to me."

Jess accompanied Agatha to the kitchen while her step-aunt was in the study. The room looked crowded. She glanced around. Tassie, Denny, and a couple of others from the farm were clustered at one end of the table. When Agatha sank into a chair, Mrs. Carter put hot tea before her. She drank it almost without tasting it.

"He ask many questions?"

"A few I didn't expect." She sketched out her answers and nudged him with her knee, under the table, when she talked about the candle.

"So that's how I could see," Jess commented. "I don't think I even knew about any candle at all. I just saw some man looming over you and plowed into him. Then I recognized O'Malley. When I saw his knife, I fought harder." His story changed smoothly. He'd have no trouble telling it to the constable.

He didn't add more. Too many ears listened. He did relay that he'd gone upstairs with the constable's men to remove the body. Denny volunteered that he had harnessed up a cart.

Then Jess' turn for evidence came. Aunt Sally didn't return to the kitchen. She declared to someone in the hall, her voice carrying, that she was retiring to her room and would not come back down until tomorrow—if then.

Denny and Tassie stayed longest. Tassie had red-rimmed eyes, but Mrs. Carter gave her no chance to express her misery. She had the woman carry tea out to the constable's men, then meat and bread, and then more tea.

The study bell rang.

"That will be for me," Agatha said.

When she entered the hall, the constable stood there, buttoning his coat.

Agatha stopped. She looked to the balcony above then at the man. "Constable Evans, is my aunt to be prosecuted for protecting me and saving Jess Carter's life?"

"The coroner's jury will decide that, Miss Helmes, but, no, I cannot see anyone blaming your aunt for her intervention."

"I am relieved to hear that."

"I find it curious, though." His narrowed eyes warned her. "Mr. Stanton Myers was killed in much the same manner. A coincidence."

Agatha stood frozen as he walked out.

Jess came back from shutting the door. He saw the horror on her face and immediately knew the cause. "He thinks your aunt killed Stanton Myers."

She had never suspected—but Aunt Sally had been so angry when she discovered that Stanton Myers knew about Agatha's pregnancy but had done nothing to marry her. "What if she did kill him?" she whispered.

He stopped before her. His hand caught both of hers and chafed warmth into them. "If she did—if, Agatha, for there is no proof—then she did it to protect you."

"But—murder?" Aunt Sally was forthright and stubborn, steadfast and loving. Agatha couldn't ask her that horrible question. She wouldn't.

But she would always wonder.

Chapter 16 ~ Saturday, 18 April

"He's still feverish," Abby Carter declared. "I don't need to check his forehead to see it. Look at him, all flushed."

"I ain't got a fever," Jem protested, but he didn't budge from the kitchen chair. When Mrs. Carter put a tisane before him, he reached for it, but his hand only cupped around the hot mug. Delilah mewled and wrapped around his feet. "I need to get on my way. Been here days longer than I intended."

"You need to go to bed. Bone-broth and rest," Aunt Sally declared. "Jess, help him upstairs. If you had been up here at the house, Jem Webb, you wouldn't be in this state now. Off in that stable with no one to watch over you. I'll make up the bed in the chamber beside Jess." Off she went, expecting obedience.

"Up you get," Jess said and tugged on Jem. The big man groaned, but he lumbered to his feet. Jess steered him toward the door. "Ma, can you bring up that cup?"

"Tassie—."

"I'll take it up, Mrs. Carter," Agatha intervened. She scooped up the tisane and cupped her hands around it as she followed the men to the entrance hall.

Their passage up the steps was turtle-slow yet steady, with Delilah pacing ahead then coming back down then repeating the pattern. Jem Webb leaned on Jess more than he would ever admit. "I need to get goin'. The ladies are nice. I don't wanna bring trouble on 'em. Three days—."

"Five days, but never you mind," Jess reassured him. "You're not leaving here with a fever and an infection. You'll lose that arm if you don't treat it carefully."

Samson joined them and tried to twine around their feet. Agatha scooped him up and held him in one arm.

Aunt Sally had quickly made up the spare bed and waited, arms akimbo, her nursing supplies waiting on a side table. Jem groaned when he saw the bandages and salves but submitted to having his boots drawn off. The older woman reached for the buttons on his shirt.

"Hey there. Stop."

"Don't argue with me, young man. You need tending. That arm

needs cleaning and a salve on it before it turns septic." She tugged at his shirt and got it off.

Before her step-aunt could move to the next step in her procedure, Agatha set the tisane in Jem's hands. "Drink this now, before it gets cold."

"Can't nobody get no rest around here, with all the orders." Then he shivered. She steadied the cup. He grimaced then downed it and handed it back. "My thanks, Miss Helmes."

Her step-aunt shooed her from the room. "Jess will give me any help I need."

Delilah came with her and raced down the steps, disappearing toward the kitchen. Agatha walked more slowly, the problem of the missing deed and will still on her mind. She had to find those documents. O'Malley had hid them somewhere in the house. He hadn't had any time to leave. They had to be here.

But where? The house was large, with unused rooms and a whole attic for hiding spaces, old furniture that should be cleaned out, trunks and boxes, large paintings that documents could tuck behind and never be seen—she would never find the will and the deed. She had searched a dozen places, obvious, not obvious, easily accessed, difficult to reach. Yet no matter what hiding place she could think of, the documents were never there when she poked her hand in.

She returned the cup to Mrs. Carter then made her way to her study. Only to find her cousin seated behind her desk, casually turning the pages in the accounts ledger.

"Richard! What are you doing here?" She left the door standing open and approached the desk. "Close that ledger. You have no right to look at it. And stand away from my desk."

"No right? When this farm is half mine." Yet he closed the ledger.

"It is not. My father left it to me outright, as his father did to him. You have no claim to Helmes Farm. Or to Helmes House."

Richard placed his flat palms on top of the ledger and looked up at her. "Your father made a simple mistake, the kind he always made. He was driven by sentiment. He should have realized that no woman can run a farm. You'll run this place into the ground. You need my hand, my steady hand, to assist you."

"Do I? I think not. You sent me three men to serve as stewards here, all of them ill-suited to the job. This farm's accounts would be in the black if I hadn't been so naïve as to trust a cousin who claimed that he merely wanted to help me. Instead, he—you! would try to ruin Helmes Farm. For what other reason would give such glowing recommendations to a drunkard and a sloth and—and—I don't know what to call O'Malley. Lecher. Drunk. Thief. All of those."

"Ah. O'Malley. Interesting that you bring him up, Cousin, when you shot him dead."

"Get away from my desk," she demanded.

The growl in her voice had more effect than her demand. It startled him. His eyes widened, but he rose and stepped away.

Agatha immediately picked up the ledger and returned it to the shelving behind her desk. She noticed that the other ledgers were still stacked in order. Richard hadn't had much time for his snooping. He probably hadn't been in the house before they went upstairs and—. She whirled to face him. "How did you get in the house?"

"The front door. You should lock it. Anyone could walk in and steal you blind."

"O'Malley took all the petty cash," she lied. "You should know better than to walk into someone's house, especially when you are not welcome."

"O'Malley," he mused. "Everyone in the village is talking of his murder."

"Not murder. Defense. He attacked me, Richard. He would have raped me."

"A gentlewoman does not speak of such deeds."

Agatha barked a hard laugh. "I'm a farmer. I speak the plain truth. He stole from me, and he attacked me."

Her cousin had a sudden gleam in his eyes. "And Jess Carter killed him."

"No. Aunt Sally did that. To defend me. When he came out with a knife, she shot him."

He rocked back on his heels. "Sally Wellesley? That old spinster? She shot and killed Reece O'Malley?"

"With her pistol. A pistol is a great leveler for women. We don't need strength. We only need deadly aim. Aunt Sally has taught me that." His eyebrows shot up, for he heard the threat she implied. Agatha folded her arms. "Go back to Ipswich, cousin. You're not welcome here."

"Or you'll shoot me? Then you will spin some yarn that a gullible constable will believe."

"Constable Evans is far from gullible. He is actually too hard to convince of a crime. Had he listened to us about O'Malley, then O'Malley would be sitting in gaol rather than lying in a coffin in the cold, hard ground."

He didn't respond to that. "What will you do if I refuse to leave? Shoot me, too?"

"We're not murderers." But the question of Stanton Myers' death raised up on its cobra-shaped head. "Go away. I don't want you here.

You've been undermining me for years. I didn't truly understand, but I do now. You want this farm. You want the house. You can't have them. My father left them to me."

"Ha!" He skirted the desk and gave her his back as he walked to the fire. "The men here won't work for you. I'll see to that."

"They'll work for Mr. Carter," she retorted.

Richard slewed around. His grin stretched wide. "I'll still win. Carter is my man."

"He is not." The retort was childish, but she didn't know what else to say.

"He's not the man that you think he is, Cousin Agatha. He's wanted for smuggling. He didn't tell you that, did he?"

"As a matter of fact, Jess did tell me. Before I hired him."

He jumped on her use of the Christian name. "Jess, is it? Just how intimate are you with him? A hired man. A rough worker. Are you as intimate as you were with that rake who gave you that child?"

"You have no right to ask that question. You have no right to make any insinuations, Richard. You are not my father or my stepfather. You have no connection to me except a distant one."

"This farm is mine." He stuck to that claim.

"You will have difficulty proving that in court. My father left it to me."

"You'll lose it soon enough when the local men won't work for a woman and demand wages you can't pay."

She thought of the missing deed and will. She didn't want him to think O'Malley had succeeded. If he thought O'Malley had taken the documents, would he try to retrieve them? Here might be a chance to recover them. She had searched and searched. She would have to empty the whole house—and even then she might not find the will and the deed. A loose plank in a room. A hiding spot behind a panel. If Richard had told O'Malley where to hide the documents, though—. Here was a chance.

She remembered Richard's letter to O'Malley. She couldn't mention it, for it mentioned the deed and the will. Yet she might shape a lie around what her cousin knew and thought he knew. "Nor will the men work for you, Richard, when they learn you had O'Malley attack me."

"Said that, did he? Before you shot him?"

"Oh, he was full of his plan to rape me and steal my money from the cash box in my room. I wonder how he knew about that cash box. You know about it. You are the only one who could have told O'Malley."

"I'm sure others knew," he countered. "All those you have invited to your bed."

The offense he intended flew wide of its mark. "I only invited one man, and Constable Evans found his bones in the steward's cottage."

Richard stilled.

"With a bullet in his skull," she added.

His shoulders twitched.

Had he killed Stanton, and Aunt Sally had not? Agatha's knees went watery. She gripped her chair's back to steady herself.

"Get me some whiskey," he demanded.

"Get it yourself."

Jess walked in on her retort. "Helmes. Dammit. What are you doing here?"

Her cousin chuckled, as if he held the trump card. "So, the traitorous smuggler enters."

His fists clenched. "What gives you right to say that?"

"You smuggled with Palmer. You betrayed me."

"I didn't betray you. You sent me to keep an eye on both your cousin and the farm."

"You knew—," he jabbed a finger at Jess, "you knew I planned to marry her."

"Marry me? As if I would accept you. That plan had no wings, Cousin."

But Richard ignored her. "You knew, Carter. How many days passed before she welcomed you to her bed?"

"She hasn't. She won't. She's a lady. Just as you ain't, suggesting that."

"Keeping it as a lure, is she?"

"Whether I'm bedding her or not, it's no business of yours." Then he winced and looked at Agatha. She might have wanted a less vulgar description, but she nodded her support.

"You are my business, Carter. You agreed to work for me. I expected your loyalty. I depended on you to keep watch over my interests. I hired you to work for me."

"Work means pay, Helmes. You ain't paid me one shiny pence. Not even a farthing. I owe you nothing."

Richard folded his arms and looked smug. "You'll sing a different tune before long."

"Going to sic Constable Evans on me?"

"I know your past, Carter."

Jess groaned audibly, prompting Agatha to leave her station behind her desk and plant herself beside him. He gave a little shake of his head when he saw her intention, but he didn't stop her. His shoulders squared up.

Richard continued what he thought was his winning argument. "I know you worked with Palmer. Yes, dearest Cousin Agatha, this man that you took into your bed, he worked with a known smuggler. What's more, he's friends with another one. Jem Webb. Where is he, by the by? Webb is supposed to be here. Did you kill him, too, the way you killed O'Malley? I heard the story you spun for that constable. The whole village has bought it, but I don't believe one jot or tittle of it."

"Constable Evans won't listen to you, Cousin Richard," Agatha insisted. "He likes evidence, and you have none."

"No one will believe you about the smuggling," Jess added. "Col. Farraday and his wife will have something to say about any accusation against me that you make."

"*And* if you bring the law in," Agatha gloated about her own trump card. "they won't just be looking at Jess. They'll want to know how you know. They will find out that you are a fence for smugglers!"

"They won't believe you."

"For sure they will because we had to take our smuggled goods somewhere. And someone got the goods carted on to London." Then Jess added the kicker. "Someone recorded a profit for brandy and silks and other goods that he's got no records in his ledgers of purchasing. You only know about me because you took the smuggled goods I brought to you. Those constables will take a look at your ledgers and open up a few crates in that warehouse of yours. They'll find all those goods from France. Along with whatever else you got crated up in there. That hole you try to dig for me will fit you just as well—and better.."

"Are you listening to this?" Richard complained. "He's admitting he's a smuggler."

"I knew, from the very first day. And you're the fence for the smugglers, Richard. Receiving the goods and selling them on, for a tidy profit. Equally guilty, dear cousin, but I am much more inclined to stand with Jess than with you."

He picked up his dropped jaw. "You'll support an admitted smuggler?"

Agatha smiled. "Don't tempt me to contact the authorities in Ipswich, Cousin. I can point them in the direction of your warehouse. You have no right to this farm, nothing that will stand in court, and no right to me. Constable Evans will be very interested in your continual claim on the farm. He will wonder if Stanton Myers was killed, all those years ago, to prevent my marriage to a man who would have stood against any claim you laid on this farm. You have always blocked any man expressing a mild interest in me. That is well known in this district, isn't it? Even the vicar would have to admit to that. How easy a step to believe that you killed Stanton Myers to prevent my marriage."

His mouth opened and closed, a fish towed out of water. "Are you—do you accuse me—?"

"Did you kill Stanton? I do believe you were in the district at the time of his death. You did not want him to marry me. That would interfere with any claim you had on the farm."

"How dare you!"

"I dare because I have just realized you have a stronger motive for his death than anyone else." She would have said more, but his reddening face had her fearing he would have an apoplexy in front of her. His hands lifted from his sides. He took a step—and Jess placed himself between Agatha and her cousin.

And Richard Helmes backed up. His hands dropped. He took deep breaths until the redness left his face. He tugged down his waistcoat and then his cuffs. Yet his scowl remained. He glared from under his beetling eyebrows. "Agatha Helmes, you are not the woman I thought you were."

She drew herself taller. "No, Richard, I am not. I am better."

Jess nudged her.

"The locals won't work for you, Helmes," he repeated his earlier argument, "not once I tell them that you hired O'Malley to hurt Agatha."

"The locals won't work for you," she added, "not when they know you threatened a defenseless woman who is your own cousin. Even the vicar will no longer be your ally. They may not believe O'Malley set fire to the cottage, but they will believe—I will say it until they believe it—they will believe you killed Stanton Myers and hid his body. They will demand Lord Chalmsley have you prosecuted for Stanton's death."

He seethed, but he made no rebuttal. Finally, he said, "I can't return to Ipswich tonight. I won't stay in Helmesford. You must offer me a room."

Agatha wanted him gone from the house and her life. Yet she had a sudden vision of spotting Richard as he pulled the documents from a hiding place. "You can stay one night," she agreed, and lest he think she had weakened, she added, "but I want you gone before noon."

. ~ . ~ . ~ .

"Why the hell offer him a room?" Jess demanded.

"Because he might know where O'Malley hid the documents."

"Ah." Jess kept his arm looped around her waist. "Aye. He must go after them tonight. And I'll be waiting."

But now that he knew about her plan, Agatha began to worry.

"What if he's armed? Jess, he's sneaky. I do believe he was the one who killed Stanton. He's that kind of person, all devious."

"Your aunt has her little pistol. Helmes won't dare get himself shot. We boxed him in with telling him that the villagers will demand he be investigated. His only chance is to destroy the documents."

"What if we didn't box him in enough? What if he thinks he can have other documents forged? And bring in false witnesses? If he makes a strong enough claim on the farm and the house—. No one will want to stand against the man who will control their livelihood in this district."

"I promise you, Agatha. Helmes knows his only option is to remove the real will and deed. He might plan to create forged documents, but not with those out there. And he has to look for those documents tonight."

"Or just walk in when we're not here. He came into the house today and we were here. He can walk in and out as he pleases."

"Not any more," he vowed and tucked her closer. "He knows we're watching now. He'll guess that we're going to lock everything up tight from now on. He can't sneak in later. Tonight he has to move."

"I'm worried."

He grinned. "I'm not. I'm beginning to see us clear of all of this."

. ~ . ~ . ~ .

Sunday, 22 March

Jess' head dropped forward. He jerked his chin up and shifted against the wall. The shushing sound of his shirt against the panel immediately froze him. He was tucked into the recessed door to the staircase leading to the second floor. If the lamps had been lit, a blind man could have spotted him. Darkness was his aid tonight.

He didn't know what watch of the night it was. Late, or he wouldn't be trying to sink into sleep. If Richard Helmes was going to head for the missing documents, he would have to move soon. He hoped Agatha had remained awake as she had promised.

He heard a soft sound, as soft as his shirt sliding against the wall. This sound came from down the hall.

Moonlight offered no help. Clouds had crowded in before dusk. Unless Helmes lit a candle to guide him, Jess would see nothing. Maybe he wouldn't need to. Maybe the man would wait and come back when he wasn't expected. Maybe—.

Light flared, looking bright in the darkness. It came from beneath a doorway. Jess held his breath and tried to count the doors. The light streamed from beneath Helmes' room. The door opened carefully, slowly, and flickering candlelight danced into the hallway.

The man crept out and walked slowly. He carefully placed each foot. The light of a single candle glowed around him, revealing his puffy face. He was fully dressed and booted and wearing a bulky coat. Once he had the documents, he would leave.

Helmes reached the landing and stopped. He stared at the family wing, dark, silent, the watchers waiting. Jess reckoned the man weighed the odds of accosting Agatha. If he killed her, he would inherit. Would he kill her? After years of carting smuggled goods to him, Jess still didn't know the man himself. He had limited any interactions with the fence. He hadn't liked his coarse jokes and his pinching ways.

Agatha wanted to believe her cousin had killed Stanton Myers. Jess wasn't sure. He didn't think the man had enough grit. But that left Aunt Sally guilty of the deed.

He would put his money on Aunt Sally. She had grit aplenty.

Helmes must have changed any plan, for he stopped staring at the darkened hall of the family wing. He glanced upward then lifted his candle high as he leaned over the banister to examine the empty entrance hall below.

And then he stepped away from the landing and approached the wall. He lifted his candle higher and held it before a painting. Paintings! In their search for the missing documents, not one of them had looked behind paintings. Jess hadn't thought of those hiding places. Agatha might have, but she wouldn't have wanted her cousin to wonder what she searched for.

Jess watched Helmes examine a landscape of the farm then move to the next, a hayfield in harvest. *Is he looking for a particular painting or is he counting to find the right one?*

Helmes set his candlestick on the little side table nestled beside the chair covered in red velvet. Then he put his hands on one of the larger frames. Carefully, he eased the base of the frame away from the wall. Holding it with one hand, he felt behind it. When he grinned widely, Jess knew the man had found what O'Malley had hidden for him.

Jess stole from his hiding place. Helmes did not see or hear him. He was unfolding the documents.

"I'll have those," Jess said.

Helmes jumped. "What the—what are—no!" His hiss gave extra vehemence to the words. "These are mine."

"Give 'em over. They don't belong to you. They belong to Agatha."

"Hush. Don't wake anyone." He held the documents to his chest, both hands splayed over them. "I'll pay you, Carter. I got a hundred pounds with me. You come to Ipswich, and I'll make it a full five hundred. Enough to set you up in business. Just let me go back to my room."

"He can't quite do that, cousin," Agatha said from behind her cousin.

Helmes whirled. When he saw the pistol in her hand, he staggered a bit. He recovered by drawing himself taller. Jess wished the man didn't stand between him and Agatha. She looked brave standing there, her hair all loose and frowsy, her robe belted around her nightgown. Helmes could attack her before Jess could stop him. Only the pistol would give him pause—and only if he believed her lie that Aunt Sally had taught her to shoot.

"Are you going to shoot me the way you did O'Malley? Two shootings within days of each other." His voice steadied as he spoke. When he wagged a finger and "tched", Jess knew that Helmes had lost his fear of the weapon. "You'll raise doubts with that constable. He will no longer accept that either shooting was self-defense."

"You hand over those documents, and I won't need to shoot you." Agatha held out her hand. Her eyes squinted at her cousin.

Jess winced. It was the wrong ultimatum, and Helmes' laugh proved it.

"You won't shoot me, Agatha. You don't have the nerve."

"I won't let you leave here with them."

He chuckled. "I don't have to keep them with me. All I have to do is ensure that you don't have them to counter any claim I make on the property."

"Lord Chalmesley knows what the will says."

"Chalmesley is getting too old to be an accurate witness. He won't remember the particulars of the deed, such as the size of the farm and where the boundaries actually run. With a little persuasion from his penurious brother—."

Agatha's mouth twisted. "I suppose Roddy Seddars is in debt to you?"

"Of course. Who isn't in this district? The magistrate needs a loan occasionally. The vicar likes the occasional run on the ponies. Roddy Seddars stays deep in debt, no matter how much his brother's man of business pays out. And I buy his vowels, only too ready to help out. I am, after all, a native of this district. I want to see everyone thrive."

"What are you going to do?"

"What O'Malley should have done before he got distracted." And he thrust the documents into the candle flame.

Jess leaped. He shoved Helmes. The documents went flying. He had one swift glance to see that Agatha had dropped her pistol to beat out the flaming papers, then he was punching Helmes.

The man had weight on him and a ruthless nerve that drove his punches, but Jess had speed and strength. Helmes knew how to fight, but Jem Webb had taught Jess how to fight dirty. He dodged a blow to his nose and bore in with punches to the gut. He danced back when the man tried to punch back. He kicked at the man's knee. Helmes howled, ensuring that no one else in the house would be asleep. Then he plowed for Jess.

Helmes grabbed him around the shoulders. Jess slipped and slid, but the man had a grip on his shirt. He hit hard, but Helmes blocked it then shoved his elbow into Jess' chest. Breath wheezing, he had sense enough to strain away and missed getting his head butted. They fetched up against the wall, and Jess got lucky, his right hand free while Helmes' was trapped against the wall. He punched hard, determined to beat the man into submission.

A lamp increased the hall's brightness. For a half-second he stared in Helmes' eyes, thinking what a pig he looked, then the man tore away from his grip. He pounded down the stairs. They heard the bolts drawn back, then the front door was flung back, and Helmes was gone.

Agatha ran to Jess. "Are you hurt? Where are you hurt?"

He set her gently aside and headed down the stairs.

Helmes was gone, running down the drive for the village.

He reckoned the man would drop to a walk as soon as he was out of sight of the house. He hoped Helmes would head back to Ipswich. Without the will, he had no challenge to the house. Without the deed, he couldn't create a mishmash of boundaries and acreage. Agatha was safe.

Jess bolted the door and headed back for the gallery. Agatha and his mother and her aunt and Jem, though, were leaning over the banister. The cats had arrived and were poking their heads between the railings.

"He get away?" Jem asked as Jess climbed the stair.

When he reached the landing, Agatha pressed close to him. Jess lifted his arm to wrap around her slim form and haul her closer. "He's heading for the village at a run."

"He needs takin' care of."

"Not murder." It was a warning.

"Nyah. Mebbe a good word in a bad ear, though."

Jess shook his head. "How much of them documents burnt?"

Aunt Sally lifted them. "A little scorched, but only a couple of corners were burned. None of the words. He won't be able to challenge anything about either of them."

"We got lucky."

"Indeed we did," Agatha said, tucked into his side. "He could have had a gun or a knife."

"But he didn't."

She looked up into his face. "Is it over?"

He felt the tremors racing through her, after-shock, he reckoned. He felt a little weak in the knees himself. It felt too quick to be over, but it was done. With the documents back, Helmes could do nothing. He was gone. He wouldn't hang around spreading half-truths and gossip when they'd told him earlier that they could spread their own truths and lies about him. The man would eventually try something for sure, once he got his feet under him again.

"We got a breathing space," he told her. "You're shivering. Time to get you back in your warm bed."

"We all should return to bed," his mother said. "Providence has worked everything to our favor, as if all of this was intended to be set up and finished off. Now, back to sleep, all of you. Especially you, Jem Webb. You're none too steady on your feet. Off with you now."

Jem grinned and headed for his room. Aunt Sally handed the documents to her step-niece, yawned greatly, then called the cats to her and pattered back to her room. His mother smiled at him then went to her own room.

Jess whisked Agatha back to her room. And when she pulled him inside after her, he didn't protest. He planned to stay.

# 1815

Epilogue ~ July

Bees dipped in and out of the rose hedge and buzzed away with pollen plumping their legs. The blue sky promised another lovely summer afternoon. After the difficult growing season of 1812, Agatha had hopes that Helmes Farm would have a third thriving year.

The baby inside her kicked, strong and healthy. Stanton Myers' child had never kicked so hard. Her little girl had kicked this hard, struggling in the confines of the womb. Little Sally continued to kick against the confines of the world.

She toddled now, trying to reach the pond before her father intercepted her. When her little gown tangled in the high grass, she pitched forward onto her hands and knees. The world knew her displeasure with her loud squawls.

Jess snatched her up and kissed her rosy cheeks. Tears forgotten, she mimicked her mother by flinging both arms around his neck.

Agatha smoothed her hand over her moving belly as she walked—waddled to meet them.

Jess' eyes narrowed. When he joined her, he set Sally on the ground and turned her toward the house. Sally, ever constant, began to veer back toward the pond.

He slipped an arm around Agatha. "Kicking again?"

"Incessantly. Give me your hand." She rested it over the current location of the heel or elbow that was determined to push into the world.

His face transformed with his wide grin. "And what will we call this one if it's a girl? Sally's taken."

Hearing her name, the little girl looked back at her parents then changed her purpose. Arms held wide, she began a tottering journey back to them. The sun gleamed in the little curls covering her head. She chuckled at her progress.

Agatha had to laugh with her. "Sally is definitely taken." She thought of her step-aunt, reduced to holding court with her cats in the drawing room. Still strong of mind, still firm of purpose, she tottered about with her cane but rarely ventured far from the house. She covered her husband's hand where it rested on her baby-filled belly. "What shall we name this one? Have you considered Delilah?"

"I'm not naming my daughter for a house-cat. Besides, Sally and Delly will never do."

"Abby?" she suggested his mother's name.

He stilled.

Sally toppled again. She started to cry. Jess started for her, but before he'd taken two steps, the little girl had discovered a wildflower before her periwinkle eyes. She rocked between her hands and knees, then sat back and reached for the flower.

He returned to Agatha and again slipped an arm around the small of her back, the only thing small about her, Agatha grumbled inwardly. "Abby for a girl. Ma will like that."

"And if it's a boy?"

"James," he said promptly. "Jamey for short."

She leaned against her husband's strong support. "Jem would like that."

"One of the things he'll never know."

Jem had left close to a month after the fateful night when her father's will and the farm's deed had been recovered. They had never heard from him, and Jess reckoned they never would. He had remained stubbornly set on the New World.

Her cousin Richard had also not contacted them again. Agatha did not know if he avoided them because of their threats to contact Constable Evans, or if the guess about Stanton's murder had hit so accurately that he feared they would discover evidence. Once she married Jess, Richard lost his easy opportunity to steal the farm.

Constable Evans had returned a few times before he left to return to London. He shared that information with them the last time he came for tea. He might have shared more, for Agatha had heard he was newly married, but Jess was too stiff. His smuggling past stood between him and the constable. Jess would never be easy around a member of law enforcement. He congratulated Constable Evans on his new position with the London Constabulary, but he would never be friends with the man.

She leaned against her husband and watched her daughter trying to grasp another wildflower in her chubby hand. She sighed with happiness. Loss had defined her, but providence gave back much more than she had lost. In risking her heart a second time, she won to joy.

The baby kicked.

Agatha smiled. She was still winning.

.~.~.~.

Thank you!

Thank you for reading ***The Danger to Hearts***. When I conceived the Hearts in Hazard series, way back in 2013, I had only a vague idea of the third book while books 4, 5 and 6 (this one) were the merest shadows. With the completion of each book, the next story's characters would start talking of their dreams and demanding their problems be confronted.

Now that book 12, *The Hazard with Hearts* is nearing completion, I am experiencing a little sadness that I will soon leave Regency England. I never expected to fall in love with every one of the books in this series, yet I have. As I have re-read them and re-formatted in preparation for their paperback publication, I have fallen in love with every story all over again.

For any questions, comments, and speculations, please contact winkbooks@aol.com. You can find my books on my Amazon author page or my website ~~ www.writersinkbooks.com

To receive monthly information about all of my books, please join my monthly newsletter list. Contact me at winkbooks@aol.com and receive a free peak of the book I am currently writing. I won't pester you with affiliate links or pass your email to any other person or institution.

Indie writers thrive on reviews. With *any* book that you enjoy, please share with other readers looking for escape from the stresses of life.

**Dream it. Believe it. Do it.**
*~~ M.A. Lee*

Hearts in Hazard by M.A. Lee

### Mysteries with a dash of romance, set during the Regency Era of England

*1 ~ A Game of Secrets ~* Smugglers, secrets and spies: Kate tries to hide in plain sight; Tony tries to catch a spy. First they fall in love, then they fall into trouble with smugglers. Will they survive?

*2 ~ A Game of Spies ~* Salons and soirées, flirtation and dancing, gambling and spies: Josette and Giles fall in love over a deck of cards—and try not to die.

Spymaster Giles Hargreaves was introduced in *A Game of Secrets*.

*3 ~ A Game of Hearts ~* **Two couples** :: One titled widow, one wealthy businessman: two hearts shadowed by their past. One bright young flirt, one hard-edged young man: two hearts crossed by circumstance. Mix in a courtesan and two rakes, all out for mischief, and murder bloody and foul.

*4 ~ The Danger of Secrets ~* Deep in the wintry countryside, a house warmed by relatives and friends: secrets of family, secrets of hearts, secrets of blood and pain. Match a daughter to an unknown father; match a spinster to an earl; match a serial killer to his next victim.

Gordon Musgrove was introduced in *A Game of Spies*.

*5 ~ The Danger for Spies ~* Impossibilities? Rakes don't lose their hearts. Spies don't give up the game. No one hides in plain sight. Codes are unbreakable. A man can't hold onto revenge for years and years. Impossibilities are designed to be shattered.

Toby Kennitt was introduced in *A Game of Spies*.

*6 ~ The Danger to Hearts ~* A country manor in early Spring: older woman and younger man. Horses, cats, needlework, roses and afternoon teas ~ What could possibly go wrong in an idyll? Trouble in the past, trouble now, and murder.

The character Jess Carter was introduced in *A Game of Secrets*. Constable Hector Evans receives his own story in *The Key to Secrets*. I have considered a story about Jem Webb in the new world. If that every occurs, it won't be part of the Hearts in Hazard series.

*7 ~ The Key to Secrets ~* Debutantes should snare fiancés, not murder them. Constable Hector Evans must solve three murders. Is his former love guilty, of is she a convenient scapegoat?

Constable Hector Evans was introduced in *The Danger to Hearts*.

8 ~ *The Key for Spies* ~ Spies and traitors. Lies and treachery. Unexpected love where bullets fly. One traitor destroys loyalty. What will two traitors destroy?

The only **Hearts in Hazard** book outside of England, *The Key for Spies* is set in northern Spain.

9 ~ *The Key for Hearts* ~ A convenient marriage inconveniently causes murder.

10 ~ *The Hazard of Secrets*. Two hearts with dangerous pasts—Can they keep their secrets, or will murder force them to reveal all?

11 ~ *The Hazard for Spies* ~ Disguised to spy. Will murder destroy their chance for love?

12 ~ *The Hazard for Hearts* ~ Two wives haunt the castle. Will she be the third to die?

M.A. Lee also writes the **Into Death** Series, set after World War I

*Digging into Death* ~ A governess seeking refuge, a handsome young man, an archaeological dig: romance is inevitable; murder is not. Suspicions escalate, artifacts are stolen, and then a second murder. Has the love of her life beguiled her straight into death? Available in paperback and e-book

*Christmas with Death* ~ Christmas is for miracles, merriment, and murder. Set in 1919 at an English country manor for a party throughout Christmastide. Available in paperback and e-book.

*Portrait with Death,* publishing soon ~ the conclusion of the Isabella Newcombe series

Nonfiction by M.A. Lee

*Think like a Pro Writer series*

***Old Geeky Greeks: Write Stories with Ancient Techniques*** ~ Storytelling has its roots in the strong foundations of classical antiquity. Avoid the re-packaged "exclusive insights" and "wham-pow webinars" and return to the source, organized as a seminar in book form.

***Think like a Pro: New Advent for Writers*** ~ Seven lessons to guide your growth from newbie writer to "thinking like a pro writer". Now available in paperback and e-book.

***Think / Pro: A Planner for Writers*** ~ An undated planner with daily word counts, progress meters, project planning, and goals analysis. Paperback only. How else will you record your goals and progress?

***Discovering Your Novel*** ~ a 52-week course for new writers, offering guidance from original idea to publication and marketing.

***Discovering Characters*** ~ Delving deeply into your primary characters entails more than just templates and character interviews. You also need to know your secondary characters. Focus on more than appearance, more than intellect, and explore your characters hearts and souls. Discover them!

***Discovering Your Plot*** ~ What writers need and want for plot structures and genre expectations. Control pacing, tension, and suspense with a stronger comprehension of the major sections of a novel.

***Discovering your Author Brand*** ~ The greatest secret to catch the attention of fly-by readers? Branding. Writers need to brand their books, their series, and themselves as the author. Packed with examples and explanations from past successful marketing efforts.

***Discovering Sentence Craft*** ~ Zeug-what? Chiasmus? Auxesis? Are those spelled correctly? Well, yes. These are literary devices used for centuries by the best writers to make their works memorable.

Writers are artists, seeking ideas from the creative muse. We're also crafters, looking for the best ways to present those creative ideas.

*DiscS~Craft* presents techniques for using figurative & interpretive concepts as well as the structures of inversions, repetitions, oppositions, and sequencings.

***Just Start Writing :: Inspiration 4 Writers, book 1*** ~Writing can be a dizzy whirl of a carousel, all colors and mirrors with unicorns and griffins and dragons to ride. How do you get your ticket, climb on the carousel, and join the writing ride? If you want to pursue your writing dream, *Just Start Writing* will help you start.

***2 \* 0 \* 4 Lifestyle: A Planner for Living*** ~ *Intermittent fasting. Bible Journaling. Keto Diet. 7-Minute Workout. Five minutes with God.* If the newest fads to follow are leaving you cold and edgy, time to re-think your daily plan. Return to Luke 10:27 to involve the whole self—heart, soul, mind & body. 2 \* 0 \* 4 offers an undated planner to help you muse and move, feast and fast, and live and love. Paperback only. How else will you write in it? Available in the Meadow and the Mountain River editions.

Pen Names of M.A. Lee

## Remi Black ~ Fae Mark'd

### The Fae Mark'd Wizard
*Weave a Wizardry Web*
*Dream a Deadly Dream*
*Sing a Graveyard Song*
*Kindle a Fae's Wrath* (coming soon)
*Quench a Dragon's Fire* (in the sketching stage)
*Dance to Bone-Edged Music* (in the sketching stage)

### Fae Mark'd World
*To Wield the Wind :: Spells of Air 1*
*To Charm the Air: Spells of Air 2* (coming soon)
*To Curse the Wyre: Spells of Air 3* (sketching stage)

Edie Roones ~ Seasons in Sansward

***Summer Sieges***
***Autumn Spells***
***Winter Sorcery***
*Spring Magicks* (in the sketching stage)

**All books from Writers' Ink are available at Amazon.**

For any comments, questions, and speculations, contact winkbooks@aol.com. Use the subject line to direct your email to a specific book or series.